Miss Humbug

Miss Humbug

STEPHANIE J. SCOTT

Cover: Melody Jeffries Design

Editing: MK Books Editing

ISBN: print 978-1-954952-18-8

ISBN: ebook 978-1-954952-16-4

Contents

Free Read

Check out my free novella **It Happened One Getaway** available to readers who join my email list. Find it here: https://www.stephan iejscott.com/free-read

Prologue

Ethan

Old habits never died. I rounded the familiar street corner and slowed my truck on instinct.

Ahead on the right, the house stood as it always had. Grand, old, proud. A Victorian with all the gables and turrets and ornate woodwork standing guard over the surrounding gentle hills and farmland. Behind the heavy double front doors, the home held secrets and mystery to most in town. But not to me.

Except one mystery. If she would ever come back. Really come back, for more than a day or two.

As I idled past, a little girl appeared in the long, curved driveway leading to the house. She spun in a circle, her pink coat like a swirl of cotton candy. Dark hair, wild and messy. Face pointed at the gray November sky.

I blinked. She was gone.

Only a memory, like everything else between us.

Chapter 1

Marlowe

I never wanted so badly to leave a place I'd just come back to.

After my flight to Chicago was canceled due to impending doom in the form of freezing rain and icy conditions, then snagging a flight from San Jose to Des Moines and managing to find the last rental car available—a giant SUV that chugged gas like a college bro drinking beer on his twenty-first birthday—I rumbled into my hometown on fumes fueled by anxiety. This was my own family and I was a nervous wreck about coming home.

Despite such a travel fiasco, nary a single snowflake covered the ground. No slick ice either. Regardless of all the brouhaha at the airport about canceled flights, the nasty weather hit north of us.

The sign for Crystal Cove came into view, a town deposited in an overlooked corner of northwestern Illinois near the Wisconsin border. A town known only to those who read travel sites for gems like *The second most popular Christmas destination in the state!*

And people believed it, the suckers.

They traveled in from places like Milwaukee and Madison and Minooka. All over they spread, clogging up the roads, leisurely strolling through downtown wearing big dopey grins, forever searching for scraps of holiday magic to absorb into their mundane lives.

Holiday magic. The very thought of magic born from holidays made me want to set something on fire.

Okay, dramatic. Get over yourself.

But for a gal who despised holidays—in particular the Christmas holidays—living in a town defined by celebrating them was a recipe that wouldn't make it into the town fundraising cookbook.

No real surprise that lack of admiration for holiday magic drove this gal away the second she was old enough to leave.

I slowed before the lowered speed limit sign came into view. Sure enough, a cop scouting for speeders lurked in the drive of the old Texaco. Rookie. The better spot was by Nash's General, a mom-and-pop convenience store whose turn-in was obscured by a bend in the road and a crop of overgrown pines.

"Nice try, Speed Trap," I muttered as the gargantuan SUV slid past at a gentle thirty-four mph.

Another mile later and I turned at the familiar road: Hollybrooke Lane. Set on a hill overlooking an honest-to-goodness valley of undeveloped land, a stately Victorian dared anyone to question its extravagance. After all these years, my breath was stolen. I loved that freaking house. As much as I'd wanted to get away from small town life, the house always brought me back.

Okay, and my family.

Us Hollys always referred to the house by the street name itself, as if we had ownership of it. Technically, the house was built by our ancestor Clifford Holly back in eighteen-something-or-rather. Only a few other houses dotted the short road, and as far as the Holly family considered, all others were an afterthought.

Cars filled the driveway in front of the over-sized detached garage. A minivan, an aging sports car, a sporty hatchback, and a sedan. And now Godzilla's Mama, the monster SUV. My family would judge me for it, calling me a West Coast Elite or Miss Marlowe Fancypants or worse. Probably worse.

I was the last one here. But I was here.

Thrusting open the car door, I slid out until my heels hit home soil.

Well, I hadn't spontaneously lit on fire, so that was promising.

"Is that little Mar-Mar?" a voice called out.

My skin boiled. "It's *Marlowe*." But the fight gave out at the sight of my oldest brother, Ashe.

His large, country-man body enveloped me in a bear hug. "You'll always be the family baby."

I took the hug. I didn't hate the hug.

He assessed me. "You look like a corporate Heidi Klum."

"Heidi Klum is blond. And a million feet tall." As a brunette notably shorter than a supermodel, we looked nothing alike.

He rolled his eyes. "Okay, *dressed* like. You better have jeans and boots because the Hollys are going out tonight after whatever Grans has in store for us. You wear those clothes and people will think they're up for audit."

Cropped black pants and classic heels were suddenly too chic? Maybe it was the tailored jacket over a silk cowlneck blouse. "Look, I *own jeans*." I scoffed but lost the war to hide my smile. "You look like you can bench press a tank. What do you do? CrossFit?"

"More like barn-fit." His chuckle caused creases around his eyes. He had a whole ten years on me, but he never seemed to change all that much between my visits. He took my suitcase without asking and I followed him through the side door. "Come on in. The kids are dying to see their cool aunt from California."

The warm air hooked me into its embrace and dotted it with a kiss on the cheek, laced with old familiar guilt.

I had nieces and nephews who knew me mainly from video calls. Those and UPS packages filled with what the parenting blogs claimed were the most in-demand gifts of the season. When you couldn't be there in person (or were possibly unwilling), piles of presents kept you close in mind.

Old polished wood and a hint of cinnamon wafted from deeper in. The house was the kind that just couldn't be recreated, and nobody would these days with all the open floor plans. Dozens of rooms all closed off from each other, with an oblong kitchen that didn't lead to a mega family room like modern houses. As a kid, I loved having so many little spaces to close myself into. The parlor, a large dining room, a library, an office, a butler's pantry, and a living space near the back of the house with a bay window overlooking the valley and a farmland of trees in the distance.

A cluster of familiar faces appeared.

"Mar-Mar!"

"Auntie Marlowe!"

Little arms reached for me as a soft arrow shot from a plastic bow and knocked me in the arm. Ashe's wife, Cara, came in for a hug, while my other brother, Shawn, gave me a head nod from across the room, not expending the effort to peel his folded arms apart. Built stocky like Ashe, Shawn stood half a foot shorter than our older brother but made up for it in attitude. We got along *great*.

My oldest cousin Rafe, a ginger-haired over-achiever, nodded to me in greeting. Where my brothers excelled at wisecracking and rough housing, Rafe seemed born to wear a suit and tie. Even as a kid his clothes stayed way too clean. His wife Brianne typed on her phone at a frantic pace, no doubt firing off orders to one of the many community board groups she belonged to. I didn't take her lack of welcome personally. She was one of those perennially busy people. Busy people got out of things like holiday dinners and whatever else I faced this weekend. All to say I admired Brianne and needed to learn her ways.

Rafe's younger sister Riley greeted me with a friendly smile. She was closest to me in age among my siblings and cousins, but still four years older. Riley had a chip on her delicate shoulder after her now ex-boyfriend left her to raise their daughter alone.

More children appeared from darkened corners. In all the calamity, my gaze landed on our summoner: Grans. She stood by the bay window looking over the side yard that sloped toward the neighboring tree farm in the distance. For a lady in her early eighties, not much slowed Grans down. And for whatever did slow her down, she had people for that.

As she shifted toward me, shadows cast witchy angles across her features. "Welcome home, Marlowe. We've been waiting."

If her welcome sounded ominous, it was because it was ominous.

The mailed invitation ran through my mind again, short and to the point in a lovely serif font on eggshell, mid-weight cardstock.

Emmaline Holly respectfully requests your presence at 21 Hollybrooke Lane for Thanksgiving dinner.

Then, in my grandmother's handwriting:

This isn't a suggestion.

Love, Grans

My grandmother never pulled rank. She could have for years, and I would have come back in an instant. In all our exchanging of greeting cards and phone calls, she never played the guilt card. She never verbally bemoaned my absence. She regularly offered understanding for my excuses for missing holidays, birthdays, and other family milestones.

I'd called as soon as I'd received the invitation. I hadn't visited in a couple years, but I wasn't a total monster. Was she...I'd dared to ask, ill? She knew how sensitive my siblings and I were about family fatality.

"Your presence is expected," had been her response when I'd asked if she was okay. "I miss you, Marlowe."

"I miss you too." And I did. That homesick feeling usually wasn't enough to derail my momentum to drop everything and travel halfway across the country for a turkey dinner.

Until work derailed on its own. Derailed—ha. More like the train tracks ended at a cliff's edge. My career's momentum crash-landed into unemployment.

I fished out airport presents for the kids—keychains, smooshy little stuffed animals, T-shirts featuring California pro sports teams. These were sporty kids. They liked sports. Just nobody ask me which ones.

The kids swarmed and scattered. I could spend face time with them later. Right now, I wanted to hear from Grans. She wanted us here, and I wanted to know why.

I crossed the room and tentatively stood before the woman who raised me. She smiled. "How was your flight?"

Terrible. "Great."

"And your job?"

Non-existent, but no way would I admit it. "Going well."

"Wonderful. I'm glad to hear."

"When is game time?" One of Ashe's kids stood holding a board game box. The cute one with freckles who wasn't sticky.

"Games are after we talk schedules with Grans," Cara answered with patience.

Adults arranged kids while I sat on the couch facing the centerpiece of the room, an ornate fireplace with a professional photo of the family mounted above the mantle. Mom and Dad smiled down at us, preserved in time. I was two in the family portrait and reaching off camera, already eager to make a break for it.

Grans made a production of sitting in a wingback chair, like a gazelle folding her limbs just so. "Thank you all for gathering. It means so much."

Calamity ensued with a shrieking child and a shushing mother, until Grans dropped the grandmother-lode. "I've decided it's time to move on from Hollybrooke House."

I couldn't have heard her right. Move on?

"You're selling," Shawn said, as a declaration, not a question. "Let me help you with the listing. No one's going to rip you off on my watch, Grans."

"No one in this town would dare," my uncle Joe piped up.

"You know, my commercial real estate company is ranked number three back home," Shawn added. "Number three and rising."

"It's not *your* company," Ashe shot back. "You just work there."

"I'm an important fixture in the line of command and—"

Grans held up a hand. "I'm not selling. I'm moving to an active, adult community with one-floor living. These stairs are killing me."

On the words *killing me,* we collectively held our breath. Look, we didn't mince words in this family. We'd been through too much.

She tossed a hand in the air. "I'm not *dying.* It's this pesky business of aging. This is too much house. After my hip surgery, the stairs have become a burden. Too many empty bedrooms with you lot off and away. The greatgrands aren't staying overnight often enough to justify keeping the rooms up. And besides, my cleaning woman is planning to retire. She's the one who showed me the lovely retirement community she's moving to with her husband."

Silence, not usually a guest in our collective presence, sank in and made itself comfortable. A pit formed in my gut. The house. The beloved house. What would happen to the house?

Grans went on. "There's not a chance I'd let the masses get in a bidding war over our beauty. This house stays in the Holly family."

Murmurs coursed through the room, which devolved into fighting among the kids, somebody crying, and loud complaining this was all so boring. See ya, Silence.

Ashe rounded up the kids and funneled them outside. "Stay in view of the window!"

Grans waited out the commotion. "Since I'm alive and kicking, there's no sense holding out on a will to pass down the house. I'd like to move ahead now. Only it leaves me with an impossible decision."

Who gets the house. Yeah, I wouldn't want to be in her orthopedic flats right now for that decision.

Uncle Joe, Grans' son, and his wife Sunny were the obvious next in line. Only they'd built a beautiful custom home they'd spent years renovating, so would they even want Hollybrooke? Ashe and Cara could be likely candidates with their three kids. Same for Rafe and his family. Or Riley and her daughter. They'd all probably appreciate owning the family legacy.

"I decided to take myself out of the equation," Grans said. "I had a brilliant idea. A contest. You're each eligible to win the house. I'm calling it *The Great Holly House Caper*."

Silence swelled for a hot second until the room exploded in noise.

Everyone talked at once. Ashe blurted a steady stream of questions as Cara spoke over him. Shawn unglued himself from the wall. "Excuse me, what?"

"Is she for real?" Rafe swung to his dad, Joe. "Why aren't *you* getting the house?"

Uncle Joe shrugged. "I'm not sure I want it since—"

"We can't compete to *win* a house," Rafe interrupted. "It's ridiculous. And weird."

He wasn't wrong.

I stood, numb to it all. Hollybrooke House was up for grabs.

Our house. My childhood home. The thought Grans would grow out of wanting the house never occurred to me.

Riley got to the heart of it, speaking directly to Grans. "A contest? Doing what?"

Grans' eyes focused on a distant point, as if she were reading a banner hanging above us. "This contest is strictly limited to the family. And while we'll be publicly participating in contest activities, no one outside of the Holly family will know the real prize. That needs to remain a secret."

A contest to win the family home *and* it was a secret?

Grans was known for harebrained ideas, like in her superglue phase when she'd repaired the garage door with the sticky stuff, and the door crushed the hood of Gramps' Oldsmobile. This idea? Clear off the map. We were in *There be dragons* territory.

"What kind of contest?" I repeated my cousin Riley's question.

Grans' eyes lit up. "I'm glad you asked. The criteria will be completing holiday festivities in town this season. I've come up with a points system and a panel of judges. The historical society, my book club, and the neighbor girl down the road will evaluate and score."

Uncle Joe's eyes bugged out. "Little Tammy Leigh? A little girl will decide who inherits a historic landmark?"

"She's nearly fifteen now," Grans countered.

The response did not lessen the confusion in the room.

"I'm taking notes," Brianne said to her husband Rafe. "I'll need details on that points system."

Didn't we all.

"How many holiday festivities do we have to complete?" Riley asked.

Grans blinked. "Well, all of them."

I pressed a hand to my forehead. Holly Days ran for a solid month with activities every weekend from now through Christmas Day. A full month of holiday festivities. Like a nightmare come true.

Not that it mattered. I lived in California and hated Christmas. Okay, hate was a strong word. I avoided the holiday like the over-hyped commercialized nightmare it was, like any rational human. Grans must have assumed I'd have no interest in the contest anyway, otherwise she'd have mentioned staying in town for a month.

Who could afford to take a month off work? Other than those who'd recently lost their job...

"Where did this *idea* come from?" Cara asked.

"A holiday movie on cable. Can you believe?" Grans chuckled demurely. "I love those small-town holiday movies. I thought, what a great idea since Crystal Cove is the state's second most popular winter holiday destination. The Holly Days festival is built right in. It's been too long since we were all together."

Eyes glanced my direction—judgy eyes. I pointed at Shawn. "He barely comes home either!"

Shawn's eyes narrowed. "Twice a year, actually. July and Christmas. Besides, what do you care? You only exist in California now."

My hands planted on my hips as I squared off with my brother. "What do you care, right back at you. You live in Tulsa."

"Tallahassee."

I glared. "I knew that." I did, I was just really flustered right now.

This was huge. Grans wasn't directly passing the house to anyone. So any Holly family member had a chance. I loved this house. I felt safe here, even though I'd avoided coming back. I cherished my memories of growing up in this home, despite often pushing nostalgia aside. It was complicated...until suddenly, somehow, it wasn't.

Grans cleared her throat. "To get us started, I'll need to know who plans to participate."

"I'm in," I said at the exact time as Shawn.

A chorus of voices responded. "You *are?*"

Ashe and Cara gaped at us. Joe discussed the update with Aunt Sunny, as Rafe informed the room that no way would any *single unmarrieds* inherit Hollybrooke House over his not-dead-but-not-willing-to-concede body. Or similar. Riley, a single parent, shoved her brother. Some things never changed.

"Why on earth would you want Grans' house?" I got out to Shawn before he could ask me the same.

He rolled his eyes. "This is an excellent piece of property. There's thirty acres out there."

"You can't sell it!" I was suddenly very invested. He had no idea how invested. I surprised myself at my own interest in investing.

"I'd keep the house," Shawn insisted. "The land is another story."

"No way." Ashe shook his head. "It's family land."

Cara emitted a low growl. "Let's not forget our history. Large swaths of this land were acquired illicitly from existing native populations." Cara taught high school history and social studies and harbored a passion for local history strong enough to impress the over sixty-five crowd at the historical society. She remained the only member of the family who could tolerate Uncle Joe's war stories—the ones he read about in books.

"This *specific* land?" Ashe sputtered.

"Have you done your research?"

She had a point. Who owned land always brought up more questions than answers in my mind, which was why I had only ever rented apartments. Okay, and also, I'd only ever been able to afford to rent. With roommates. I lived in one of the most expensive areas of the country. I figured I'd live lean a few years, then up the corporate ladder I'd climb.

Turned out the ladder was more like a step stool. And I'd managed to swing my foot past the step entirely.

The Hollybrooke House was the only real home I'd ever known. My parents had both passed on before my memories of them fully formed. Within a year of the family portrait currently watching over us. At Christmas. I couldn't prove it, but my parents' eyes looked disapprovingly over the family squabbles playing out in front of them.

"The deed is in our family name," Ashe was telling Cara. "It's a legal document."

Steam emitted from Cara's ears. "Are you *explaining* land deeds to me? I know what they are. My problem is with systemic erasure and this entitled sense of ownership people believe they have."

They continued to bicker. I dug Cara's commitment, but I couldn't let them distract me. "I want the house too. It's important to me."

Shawn scoffed. "You're a Scrooge. You can't handle a month of holiday activities."

"Scrooge is miserly," I fired back. "I'm not miserly. If anything, I'm more of a humbug."

"Semantics."

"Forgive me for not hauling out the holly the second my plane landed," I snapped, fully intending my play on words with our family name. "Grans asked who is in, and I'm in."

Rafe sneered my direction. "I'm shocked you're away from your precious job at all right now."

If only I had a precious job to return to. I opened my mouth to say as much and...couldn't. Making a name for myself became my entire reason for staying away as long as I had. That goal had driven me.

And then I hit a wall. Shock hit every time I thought of the recent job loss. *Just get another one*, the logical part of my brain argued.

I hated to admit I hadn't exactly been continuously joyful in my chosen career of supply chain management with an MBA cherry on top. As much as I loved data and the joys of organizing it, the happiness I believed logistics and operations analysis would bring me simply...didn't. And if my career didn't fulfill me, which I'd invested in at the expense of literally everything else, how could I admit that out loud? To the people I most wanted to impress?

Because everyone in my family was impressive. That was the problem. I'd always been playing catch-up to them in some way. Always looking at how to define myself apart from the accomplishments of the Hollys who came before me.

"Come on, Mar." Shawn's tone came across less harsh than Rafe's. "You don't even live here."

"You don't live here either," I told Shawn.

My youngest brother, back to folding his arms, turned up his chin. "I can work remotely. I've racked up thousands of frequent flier miles. If I have to leave, I'll be back in time to show off my three-tiered German chocolate cake at the Tasty Bake."

Okay, he was fighting dirty with the family cake recipe. Also, Tasty Bake?

"It's the name of the Holly Days' baking competition," he added, despite my not having asked. I guess my clueless expression outed me.

I hadn't thought ahead to what we'd have to do for the competition. The baking, the lights, the merry-everything. All of which I loathed. Why celebrate a time so terrible for all of us?

It hadn't always been that way. But year after year, the whole month of December grew darker for me, until I wrote it all off and swore I'd never celebrate the bloated holiday again. It became my thing. Being anti-holiday in a town revolving around that very industry. My siblings didn't carry the same baggage I did about the holidays. Or they'd gotten over it. Somehow.

"We're not interested in the game," Uncle Joe stated. "Or owning the house. Let it go to the next generation."

Ashe broke away from his wife's detailed and persuasive argument on land theft to tell us they wanted the house. Cara shook her head, her mouth in a firm line, and left the room. Ashe muttered, then followed.

Shawn clapped his hands together. "At least one down."

I threw up my hands. "You guys have houses already. And the taxes alone..." Yeah, I'd get them on the taxes. Taxes had to be a lot for a house this size.

"Please tell me the total of the most recent tax bill for this house or one you've paid." Shawn's gaze nailed me to the wall. "I'll wait."

I glared at him again because I couldn't answer and he knew it. "I'm the youngest. I spent the most time in this house."

That shut him up. I'd been raised by our grandparents the longest. I'd spent nearly the entirety of my childhood here. Shawn was eight years older than me, Ashe ten years older. My memories of Ashe were a blur of him coming and going, playing high school football, and visiting when he returned for college breaks. I was younger than both cousins, who had spent most of their summers here, but had their own homes outside of town.

"But you hate it here," Riley stated.

Until this moment, I'd vowed to never live in Crystal Cove again. The town always felt too small, too steeped in a tragic family story people refused to see past. The sad little girl whose parents died in a freak car accident on the icy interstate. *And so close to Christmas*, they'd always tag on. As if sudden loss of both parents was somehow worse when tied to a commercial holiday.

Three kids left with no parents. Though of course we'd had family. We'd had Grans and Gramps—may he RIP. We had their enchanted castle house with so many rooms to dream up new adventures. I loved the house, but the idea of living here forever and always had me feeling trapped.

Did I actually want this house?

Knowing the house would change hands, and having my career go down in flames all at once, it was too freaking much. I needed a second to think. My best practice had always been to never make big decisions while high on emotions.

Too bad my best practice resulted in a lay-off anyway. And besides, what did I have to lose if the determining inheritance factor wasn't lineage—of which I was last—but holiday festivities?

Oh, right. I hated holiday festivities.

I was doomed.

Chapter 2

Ethan

This was my season to shine. Holiday time.

"You know, I run a Christmas tree lot," I told the woman who'd squeezed into the space beside me at the bar. With glossy auburn hair and long eyelashes, she looked like a celebrity. Maybe an influencer or a model. Not a townie or I'd have recognized her. She called out her drink order to the bartender loud enough to be heard over the blaring music.

She finally noticed me. "Did you say something about a Christmas tree?"

I nodded. "Name's Ethan. Sawyer. I run the tree lot over by the highway." I cringed. My opening was rusty this early in the season. "I run a tree farm."

"Oh, that's so sweet." Lights from above the bar sparkled in her mossy green eyes.

Yup. Still got it.

I played up a casual laugh. "I know, it sounds like one of those holiday movies on TV, but it's real. I really do run a Christmas tree farm. Family business."

Her obvious delight—smile, nodding with interest—fueled me further. "We're big supporters of the Holly Days festival. We show up to most of the town events." Ladies loved this stuff. The quaint small-town vibe, the sheer holiday-ness of all of it.

A square-faced dude in a sweater with a designer logo approached and slung an arm around her shoulder. He whispered in her ear, making her giggle. The green-eyed beauty returned a whisper, completely ignoring me.

Her drink order arrived. She swiped the tall pint, turning my direction. She blinked at me and tapped the dude. "Oh, hun, this is Evan. He runs a Christmas tree lot. Like in the movies!"

"It's Ethan," I stammered, as the two gazed lovingly into each other's eyes.

They promised to stop by the tree lot while visiting her parents for the weekend. Their first holiday together.

Beside me, a snicker of laughter grew louder. "Got it on video. Bro, that was *peak* failure."

I jabbed my younger brother, Rob, with my elbow.

"Ow!"

Right in the ribs. "Did you get their consent to film?"

Rob scowled. "You ruin everything."

Did I ever. I shook off the increasing sense of dread I'd felt since leaving the farm's office. If we didn't make big moves to expand the tree farm and widen our distribution, we'd be another sad story of a small business who couldn't keep up with the times.

Rob patted me on the back. "Hey, for real, though. I know you're stressed. Worry later. I made you come out tonight to have fun."

Fun. A word I used to know the meaning of.

Checkers Bar and Grille was stuffed to the rafters the night before Thanksgiving. That's when Crystal Cove filled with folks returning from wherever they'd moved on to. Before the big Thursday meal with their families, they came in ready to drink and reminisce. I'd never left Crystal Cove, so the wider world coming to me was all super convenient.

I mean I'd *left*, but only ever temporarily. With my buddy Nick having gone off to the big city of Chicago, my annoying brother served as my wingman. Even if I insisted I didn't need a wingman.

Most of the faces were familiar. The townies were largely paired up: married with kids, married no kids, or raising a kid on their own. Which counted as paired, to me. I didn't have much luck with the single mom crowd. I could admit it—I'd maybe been a little on the immature side until recent years.

Look, I was trying. Getting the family business in order held top priority now. Honestly, the last thing I needed in my life was a brand-new relationship, no matter how loud my mother hinted she didn't want to be an old grandmother. Weren't all grandmothers old?

Yeah, I'd gotten a hefty dose of the Sawyer family stink eye for that one. Never tell a mother of any age she is old. I still had lessons to learn.

"Hey." Rob pierced an elbow into my side. Jerk. "The Holly brothers just came in."

I looked toward the door, seeing Ashe and Shawn, both burly and brawn in their own ways. They were practically royalty in this town, despite the average clothes.

And...oh. Was that? No, it couldn't be.

My breath left my body.

"Dude, watch it," Rob, or somebody, said. I couldn't tell because I couldn't see straight. I stumbled off my barstool and gawked like a ninth grader.

"It's Marlowe." The words fell out. I couldn't believe my eyes. Marlowe Holly came home.

Rob craned his neck to see past Ashe's huge frame. "No way. Are you, like, still obsessed with her?"

Brothers. Who needed them? "I'm not *obsessed.*"

Okay, I'd always been...*into* Marlowe. Big time. I hadn't seen her live and in person in years. I'd only heard updates about her through my parents.

She tugged at the collar of an oversized University of Wisconsin Madison sweatshirt—where her brother Ashe went to school. Slim jeans and...cowgirl boots? I never knew Marlowe to rock a country look.

Marlowe's face appeared more angular now, but with the same small, cute nose betraying her steely expressions. No one with that cute a nose could be truly cold-hearted. She had her dark hair pulled into tight ponytail, different than how she used to let her wavy hair hang loose. Her eyes scanned the room with a precision to rival a Terminator.

She was as gorgeous as ever. Even more so. She could wear a grain sack and she'd still draw all the attention in the room.

"You gonna talk to her, or what?" Rob's voice came like a fly buzzing in my ear.

Talk to Marlowe Holly? One did not simply walk up to Marlowe Holly and *talk.* She was no longer the girl next door to the tree farm (literally). She was a full-grown woman.

I felt like a middle schooler all over again. Around age eleven, something had shifted and Marlowe wasn't just the neighbor kid, but had become a girl...of interest.

Before I could clear my head fog, a large body in plaid invaded my view. "Sawyer boys. What's up?" Ashe Holly held out his fist for a bump.

Rob responded like a normal, functioning human. I stared past Ashe to the figure behind him.

Shawn laughed. "Yeah. She's here. Can you believe it?" He nudged Marlowe forward.

She eyerolled at her brother and pasted on a smile. A fake one. "Hey, guys. How...have you been?"

Since my brain didn't work, Rob did the talking. Whatever he said was fine. Why was I such a mess? Marlowe was just a person.

Just a person I'd spent ninety percent of my teenage years dreaming about. About fifty percent of my childhood actually spending time with. And still had zero idea how to ever tell her how I felt.

Teenage Marlowe Holly had been untouchable. A mystery. I'd had all-access backstage passes to the famed Holly family growing up, but things shifted over time. We all used to be close. Me, her brothers, her cousins. Long summers tearing through the Holly property bordering my family's tree farm. Running around in the big Hollybrooke House. Being there always felt fun and exciting. A little like magic.

"Glad to see you back," Rob said to Marlowe. When had he developed social skills? Usually his headphones were glued to his head. "How are you?"

"I'm great!" Marlowe spoke loudly to be heard over the crowd and music.

"A table's clearing out." Ashe gestured ahead. "Let's grab it."

The Holly brothers herded us into the dim depths of Checkers. Marlowe hesitated. I shook sense into myself. Something must have happened with the family. Why else would she be here?

"Are you okay?" I asked Marlowe.

Her gaze refocused. "Ethan." She said my name slowly, like it was coming back to her from a distant memory. She smiled again—still a little plastic, but not as artificial as before. "It's been a long day. I can't believe they convinced me to come out tonight."

We slowly made our way to the table, which didn't have enough chairs for all of us. "You live in California now, right?"

A spark emerged in her eyes. "How did you—of course you know. Our family business is everybody's business in this town. How could I forget?"

This town was all I knew, so I didn't have much of a response.

Rob gestured toward us. "Mar, take my chair. You look tired."

Marlowe winced.

Dude. Never tell a woman she looks tired. I'd learned that one the hard way too. "He's young and green," I told Marlowe. "Also dumb."

"I heard that." Rob pulled the chair out for Marlowe.

Another extra chair miraculously appeared from a table nearby. Everyone sat and talked at once. The novelty of seeing Marlowe still struck me dumb. Here. In our town. If she'd returned home at all since college, she'd kept close to the family house, because I hadn't seen her.

"Maybe she's gone off the deep end," Ashe was saying to the table. "But we need to keep this focused. The house should be ours."

Shawn folded his arms. "Your wife doesn't seem on board with your plan."

"She doesn't want to clean all those bathrooms." Ashe leaned back in his seat. "I'll clean them."

Marlowe laughed. "No, you won't."

Ashe pretended to look offended. "Hey. I'm your elder here. I've been a homeowner for longer than you've been an adult."

I needed to backtrack. "What's this about the house? Is Mrs. Holly...she isn't..."

The Hollys had lost so much. If Emmaline was losing her health—I couldn't even say it.

"Grans is fine," Marlowe stated. "We might as well tell them," she said to her brothers. "You already talked around it."

Ashe leaned in. "This doesn't leave the table, Sawyer." He and Shawn always called both me and Rob by our last name. "You two are about as close to family we've got. Grans is giving up the house."

"To one of us," Shawn added.

"Through a *contest*." That last bit came from Marlowe. "She watched some sappy holiday movie while recovering from hip surgery. Now she has this wild idea to have her grandchildren compete to inherit the house."

I was pretty sure my jaw hung open. Rob's nose scrunched, clearly as confused as me. "What kind of competition?"

"Get this," Marlowe said. "She's using the Holly Days festival. Like, the bake sale and the snowman games or whatever. All that holiday crap."

"Some of us *like* that crap." Ashe gave her a superior look.

"As if you're out there building snow people and making gingerbread houses." Marlowe scoffed. "Your kids do those things. Not you."

"And how would you know?" Ashe challenged.

"I've seen pictures."

A server came by to take drink orders. I barely heard her. The Holly house was changing hands. The house with land backing up to our Sawyer family tree farm. The farm we desperately needed to expand to stay competitive.

The Hollys consistently refused offers on their land. Emmaline Holly loved Crystal Cove, but she loved her family estate more. My parents weren't shrewd business types and would never dream of driving a hard bargain with someone they respected so much. So the tree farm stayed small. Manageable.

In recent years, Dad's back surgeries never seemed to relieve his constant pain. Mom said she'd let the whole farm go if Dad would only agree, but he was stubborn. He was hanging on, but with no new ideas on how to revitalize the business. And he sure didn't seem interested in my ideas.

Rob took side gigs playing covers at bars and local festivals. He played guitar, had design skills, and basically was good anything else other than farming. I couldn't see him sticking around much longer. Which left me to figure out how to keep the farm running.

"And for you?" The server waited on my order.

"I'll have the local winter ale on tap." My head buzzed with ideas. There was something here. Something big.

"Winter ale, eh?" Marlowe spoke at my general direction as Rob and her brothers were wrapped up in another conversation. "You always were a *festive* guy."

"I love Christmas—what can I say?" I shrugged. "Hey, so, what's the deal with this house competition? It's you three against your cousins? What about your aunt and uncle?"

She took in a breath. "My aunt and uncle passed on taking the house and said it's up to the grandkids. And it's not the three of us versus them. It's everyone for themselves."

"Except you, right? So, your brothers against the cousins?"

She gave me a sharp look. "I want the house."

"You...want Hollybrooke House? You realize it's in Crystal Cove, right?"

Her look turned steel-edged. "I do understand geography, yes."

"Right, but like. It's here. And you live in California."

She sat straighter. "Maybe I don't anymore. Or won't. I don't know. Life changes."

My thoughts ran sideways. "So, you're in competition with each other? What would you even do with the house?" And all that land?

It wasn't like she had a growing brood of kids like Ashe or real estate experience like Shawn. Wait—what did I actually know about the current day Marlowe Holly? Maybe she owned a business. Maybe she had kids and a spouse on the West Coast. Did Marlowe get married? Did she marry some billionaire?

"I...actually don't know yet," she admitted. "But I'm not letting anyone take the house without a fight." She looked me over. Assessing. "Actually, I have an idea. I think you might be exactly what I need."

Chapter 3

Marlowe

Ethan was here. *My Ethan.*

I couldn't actually call him *my Ethan*. Not after so many years of dropped contact with my oldest friend.

Schmoozing at Crystal Cove's sad excuse for nightlife after traveling halfway across the country was not my idea of a good time, but running into Ethan Sawyer felt fortuitous. Maybe even downright miraculous.

I nudged Ethan's beer bottle with my own, causing a light *clink.* "Let's go outside."

Ethan nodded and stood.

"Don't let her take off," Ashe called after us.

"*Let* me," I grumbled. "I'm my own person."

And being here in Crystal Cove meant I wasn't. My own person. Yup, I'd had to hightail it out of town to become something other than an interchangeable piece of the famed Holly family. Once wealthy, but not immune to tragedy. We were the cautionary tale that money couldn't fix everything.

A line of smokers and vapers gathered outside. I veered the opposite direction, which offered a dark but pleasant view of evergreens. I stamped my feet to get my circulation going.

Ethan nodded toward me. "Nice boots."

I snickered. "Courtesy of Cara, Ashe's wife. I feel ridiculous."

"You don't look ridiculous."

A familiar shyness hit instantly. "Um, thanks." Subject change incoming! "Hey, I'm sorry you got sucked into our weird family drama." And my life, period. "Probably not what you were looking for tonight." I shivered into my borrowed sweatshirt which was warm but not warm enough.

Ethan peeled off his coat. "Here."

"No, you don't have to—" Warmth spread over my shoulders. "You didn't have to do that." But I was glad he did.

"Sawyer blood boils. We run hot. Always have."

I laughed. A real laugh that felt freeing after today's tension of travel and a bananas family competition. And who was I kidding, tension that had built for weeks. Months. Even longer. "Why do we constantly self-identify as our family names? I started referring to myself as a Holly the second I got back."

"I'm used to it. I answer to Sawyer same as Ethan."

I knew this and yet I had to hear it again to remember.

I didn't know how to do this anymore. Talk to people who'd known the Crystal Cove version of me but knew nothing of who I'd become. Especially, of all people, Ethan, who I'd known for so long. I supposed if I was really aiming to win the family house, I better get good at remembering the Crystal Cove version of me.

"So, Ethan. Growing up, you were pretty into the Holly Days fest. Are you still?"

"Yeah, absolutely. Every year I'm there." His whole demeanor shifted, now more relaxed. "We use Holly Days to advertise the tree farm and the Christmas tree lot."

"Your family still runs the tree lot?" Perfect.

"Yeah, I work at the farm full time. My brother part-time."

Perfect on top of perfect. "I wasn't sure if you were only in town for Thanksgiving."

His cheeks reddened. "Nope. Not all of us have big dreams like you."

Big dreams ending in...whatever state I was in now. "I'm a bit out-of-the-loop on the whole Holly Days thing. If I want to be competitive, I'll need help."

He nodded, waiting. Watching.

Right. I needed to actually ask. Ask him for help. Why was this so hard? "So, um. Could you maybe refresh me on the whole holiday festivities thing? Give me some pointers?"

His smile appeared eager. "Whatever you need, I'm your guy." He breathed easily, not seeming cold in the slightest. "I'm surprised you want the house, is all. I'm surprised to even see you here. Especially since the holidays are, well, not your favorite."

For obvious reasons. The very reason I avoided frequent visits to Crystal Cove. Often, I chose to come back in the summer, where I went camping with Ashe and the family, or tagged along on day trips with Grans. Sometimes I'd visit old friends in nearby areas or in Chicago, limiting my time in town.

A whirlwind of emotions surged. I could hardly make sense of myself right now, let alone explain my shifting outlook to another person. I wasn't ready to dish all my details to Ethan, but one thing I knew. I could trust him. I could always trust Ethan.

A memory hit and nearly knocked me over. Fourth grade, gym class. Mickayla Abernathy shoved me when the teacher wasn't looking.

"You can't be on my team," she'd said. "Your parents are dead."

As if this logic made any sense for elementary school team-based fitness bingo, but my still-developing brain had no idea how to counter it.

I'd stared at the gym floor, feeling as miserable as she'd hoped I would. She was right. I had dead parents.

Other kids visibly shrank back. Uttering the words *dead* and *parents* together had the desired effect.

"Shut up, Mickleberry Abercrombie," my knight-in-gym shorts hero, Ethan Sawyer, fired back.

(He'd actually just been wearing his regular clothes since we didn't change for gym in elementary, but my memory could be whatever it wanted.)

The clapback wasn't even offensive, but it also had the desired effect. Mickayla got mad.

Every comeback she'd thrown down, Ethan returned with a zinger. A small crowd gathered until our P.E. teacher realized we weren't flexing bingo strategies but entrenched in an outright Who's the Dummy Now? war.

Ethan was shunted off to the principal's office. Mickayla got moved to another team. She'd *hated* that. And my guts, it turned out.

All because my parents dared not to exist anymore. Because I'd had the misfortune, in her eyes, of living with my kooky grandparents in the creepy old house on the hill on a nearly deserted country road. Mickayla lived in town in a split-level ranch with an attached garage. I didn't care much about houses then, but I knew enough to know where I lived, and my life in general, was different. And different was bad.

Ethan never treated me like a curiosity when he came to our house. He played our games, was an ace at capture the flag, and didn't gang up on me like Shawn and my cousins. Or treat me like the family baby.

Ethan was a good guy. And I planned to use him to get what I wanted.

"Hey, you okay?" Ethan asked, present day.

"Yeah, sorry. The nostalgia hits in waves. It's brutal." I laughed as cover. Too real. Too much.

"It's got to be hard coming back." He studied the outlines of hardened footprints in the mud. "I'm glad you're here. For however long, and for whatever reason. It's good to see you."

Ethan had grown since I'd last seen him. His shoulders had broadened, his face had angles, and light scruff dotted his chin. The boyishness was gone—except when he smiled. He had an easiness about him, which set him apart from the guys I knew in San Jose. Corporate guys whose casualness took significant money and sculpting time at the gym. I didn't see Ethan as a gym guy. Maybe at the farm, he log-lifted.

Focus. The house.

I needed to aim everything I'd once spent on my career into this task alone. I'd figure out the rest later. "I was actually thinking, just now, maybe we go for more of a solid partnership. Beyond tips and things. You could be the essential piece I need to win this competition."

He opened his mouth, then closed it. Opened it a second time. Stared into space. "I had an idea too. About this arrangement."

"Of course."

He rubbed his hands together, seemingly less from the chill and more to get the idea stimulated. "I'm looking to expand the family business. Every year, we barely keep up with the demand despite planting on every square inch we've got. My folks, I don't think they have it in them to take on more. If I help you and if you win, I want to buy a portion of Holly land to expand our farm."

I blinked. Blinked again. Ethan...was asking to buy Holly land. The Hollys never gave up land. Ugh, there I went again referring to us as the collective Hollys. This was about *me*. If I owned the house, I could do whatever I wanted with the land. Unlike Shawn, I wouldn't sell it to some skeezy condo developer. No way. But parceling out a chunk to another longtime Crystal Cove family? That didn't sound bad. Then I'd have income to live on while I did the rest of the figuring out stuff.

"You have money to expand?" The plan was no good if he assumed I'd hand over the property for a nickel and a smile.

"We've got a good relationship with the bank. I put together a business plan. It's sort of a sore spot with my parents—they're not on board with expanding. Yet. This could change everything."

Wow, Ethan had his act together more than I'd expected. It made sense he'd want something in return for helping me.

"I'll have to consult the land deed." Hopefully, I sounded legit. In my world, deeds were good or bad, not *land*. I still felt uncomfortable with the idea of owning land, beyond the house at least, let alone selling it.

And here I'd thought we were merely coming out for a drink and a few laughs.

"Deal." I refused to overthink this. I needed Ethan's help, and with him invested for his own reasons, well, that was a dollop of terrific on top of a sundae of perfect.

We shook hands. A burst of heat shot up my arms. My cheeks absorbed the impact. I was *blushing*. From *touching Ethan*.

Okay, so this was new. Really new. And strange. And different.

I cleared my throat. "We should keep the reason for the partnership quiet. You know, from my brothers and cousins. Is that cool?"

He shrugged easily. "Sure."

I smiled at Ethan, grateful to be back to the deal at hand. The hand I'd shaken which resulted in a blushstorm. Whew—this was going to be quite the vacation. "I think we'll make a great team."

Chapter 4

Ethan

I stood on the front porch on Hollybrooke Lane. I couldn't remember ever using a doorbell here and didn't see one, so I lifted the fancy brass knocker and hit it against the ancient door. And waited.

The door swung open to nothing. I looked down. A kid emerged on all fours. "Rowl?"

"Uhh…"

The boy, freckled with shaggy brown hair, tilted his head. "Woof woof, rowl?"

An older boy appeared behind him. "He thinks he's a dog. It's been happening since Tuesday."

I crossed the threshold, pumpkin pie in hand, stepping over the child-dog who had since rolled to his back with legs in the air, panting.

Children's squeals and the sound of a blaring TV tuned to the big game floated toward me as I made my way in. Not much had changed. The loudness, the family portraits in the front hall, the heavy chandelier dripping with crystals dulled by dust and age. The full, upright suit of armor where we stuffed gum wrappers into the helmet's eye holes.

"Ethan." Marlowe stood in front of me, smiling.

Dangit, I'd forget my own name looking at her smile.

Truth, I'd had my doubts about this partnership since our talk last night. What would her family think if they knew I wanted a chunk of their heritage? They'd think I was using Marlowe.

Maybe I was.

But seeing her smile, well, I sort of didn't care about anything else.

We entered the kitchen to a mix of adult Hollys. Everyone talked over each other about oven times, the football game, and whether the Holly Days fest actually began this weekend or next.

"It's officially this weekend," I answered.

A hundred eyes turned toward me. Okay, not a hundred. A lot. All of the eyes.

"Why, is that Ethan Sawyer?" Emmaline Holly herself approached me with open arms. She stood taller than most of the women her age in town. Pale skin that wasn't weathered from sun and wind like my family of farmers.

I accepted her hug. A tight one—the woman was strong. "Hello, Mrs. Holly."

"Oh, yeah, we met up with Sawyer last night." Ashe popped a cracker coated in cheese dip into his mouth. "Mar-Mar—did you invite him?"

Emmaline made a *tsk tsk* sound. "It doesn't matter who invited him. Sawyers are always welcome here. Tell me, how are your folks? I haven't seen them around lately."

I filled her in with the basics. Which did not include Dad's back issues, Mom's health concerns for her own parents, or Rob's increasing disinterest in the family business.

"They're great," I summed up.

She paused, looking at me, like the old days when I swore she could read my thoughts. "Wonderful." She returned to her pot on the stove. "Your pie can go in the dining hall."

"The dining *hall*," Marlowe whispered to me in a haughty voice. She cracked a sly grin. "Who else on earth calls their dining room a hall?"

"I heard that," Emmaline said. "It's stately."

Marlowe led me by the arm into the far less crowded dining room. The room *was* big.

She snatched the pie and tossed it on the buffet table lining the wall.

"Hey, careful. That's homemade."

"Sorry. Look, we need to strategize. I didn't realize the festivities started this weekend. We were all arguing about it. What happens this weekend?"

Her hair was in one of those messy styles where pieces stuck up and out from a bun. Something told me it was less a look and more a result of the overall chaos.

"Light Up Crystal Cove is Saturday night in town square. It coincides with the Holiday Haus opening. Then, Sunday afternoon is the all-town volunteer."

She squinted at me. "I'm going to need you to translate."

I leaned against a chair at the table. "Saturday is the tree lighting in town square—"

"Tree lighting, meaning, just like, putting up the lights on the big pine tree?"

"No, turning them on." How did she not know this? "A crew already put the lights on. It takes them days."

She made a face. "Okay, so looking at a tree turn on, got it. What's a holiday haus?"

"The German-themed outdoor market. You really don't remember any of this?"

"You're forgetting I avoided Holly Days from the moment I was allowed to stay home. I basically holed up in my room every December or hung out in Shelby VanHorden's basement."

Oh, how I'd wished back in high school I'd been invited to Shelby VanHorden's basement. I'd wanted to be anywhere Marlowe went.

She coughed. "Anyway. What's the volunteer thing?"

"Ah, well that's actually newer. It's a big round-up of projects at local businesses in the area to encourage folks to try out a volunteer assignment. It's good advertising for the businesses. Often they get steady volunteers from it. It's how I got into building houses."

Her eyes softened at the edges. "You build houses?"

"For a charity, yeah. I'm a small part of a team, so it's not like I'm a general contractor or anything."

She studied me with her sharp gaze. "You underestimate your skills. You always have."

I wanted to deny it, but Marlowe knew me pretty well. Her years in California aside.

"I'm good at some things, sure." The room grew hotter. Maybe the turkey heat from the kitchen was drifting in.

Marlowe spun and walked toward the door. She abruptly turned back. "Okay. Volunteering definitely matters. I can do that. Do you have a list of the volunteer places? My brothers haven't mentioned this at all. They probably already have their gigs lined up."

I took my phone out. "The animal shelter is always first to book up. But there's a respite care house—that's for kids with disabilities or emotional needs. And the food bank, the park district—"

"The respite one. I'd like to go there. Is it full?" She peered over my shoulder, her warm breath welcome against my neck. My body progressed from simmer to an emerging boil.

Get a grip, dude. "I'll check."

She backed away. "I don't know why I'm acting so helpless. I can sign myself up. What's the website called?"

"Remember Mrs. Bartek, our Earth Sciences teacher? She runs the Facebook group used to organize the volunteering. I'll check the latest posts." I found the group and a pinned post with a link to a spreadsheet. "Do you want me to join you, or is that not part of the deal?"

"What deal?" Shawn Holly appeared in the doorway. He couldn't help himself wearing a tight, short-sleeved shirt to show off his arm cannons. Eh, I could take him in a fight. I hauled around trees for a living.

Marlowe moved a spare chair from the corner and squeezed it between two place settings. "Ethan is helping me get re-acquainted with Holly Days."

Shawn made a production of sniffing the air. "I smell a rat. You up to something?"

"Not any more than you," she said lightly.

Shawn pointed at me. "No cheating, Sawyer."

I threw my hands up. "I don't even know the rules. I'm just here to—" Why was I here again? Oh, right. I wanted something from them. Something my family had wanted for a good long time. I wouldn't let that loose for free. "Hang out with Marlowe," I finished. "We've been planning this for a while."

Well, that slipped out.

Shawn and Marlowe turned to me, both wide-eyed. Shawn looked at Marlowe. "You and Sawyer have been keeping in touch?"

"I, we—" she stammered.

My mouth—why?

"Wait, I get it. Mar-Mar, you were acting all shy and tongue-tied when you saw Sawyer at the bar. You two ran off for a while. Is he why you came home? You and him? He and you?" He pointed between us, grinning. "Yeah, I get it. Don't worry." He made a zipping motion across his mouth. "I won't say *nothing*."

Marlowe pressed her lips together in thought. She shot me a helpless look. "Yeah, you caught us," she told Shawn. "We were hoping to keep it, you know, low profile for now. Not make it a big deal to the family."

Shawn's eyes lit with understanding. "Long distance is tough. Remember I tried long distance with Jenna? She lived in Fort Myers and I'm up in the Florida panhandle. Too far. In the panhandle, we take care of ourselves."

I had no idea what he meant, but he'd moved off the topic of me and Marlowe, so that was a plus.

Moments later, the room filled with more Hollys, picking at the appetizers and obsessing over when the big meal would be ready.

Marlowe slid next to me, and it was as if everyone else disappeared. "Don't sweat this. We'll talk more later. I have an idea."

Chapter 5

Marlowe

The rest of Thanksgiving Day passed relatively painlessly. Usually, my relatives were a total pain. Ethan chatted with the Hollys as if only weeks had passed since we'd last been all together. As a result, I found myself relaxing. Even having fun.

The herculean post-Thanksgiving task of cleaning up became a game with Ethan. Like we'd done as kids, we instituted timed "dish sprints" to see how fast we could wash and dry a stack of plates (Grans' good holiday dishes required handwashing). Then the silverware. The oldest nieces and nephews tackled the dishwasher items while the adults bickered over how to best sort the leftovers.

It struck me how I'd never graduated from dish duty. Dish duty was solidly a Holly kid task. With Ethan around, I felt less annoyed by the reminder.

After all, another idea brewed to distract me.

Dark settled in by the time Ethan headed out. I walked him to his truck. "I can't believe you baked a pumpkin pie yourself. From a real pumpkin."

"Pumpkin is just another type of squash."

As if that fact made pie creation from vegetables any more tangible. "I buy my squash frozen and already cubed. Or plastic. For decoration."

"You buy decorations?"

Dang, he was sharp. "No."

Reality check: with the Tasty Bake competition coming up, I would need Ethan more than ever.

He rubbed a hand across his chin. "So about what I told Shawn, about us planning this time together. I—"

"It's perfect."

He blinked. "It is?"

I rubbed my arms for warmth. "Shawn filling in the blanks made me think. Not only does us dating cover for our arrangement in case anyone asks why you're around so much, it also gives me credibility with my family for the competition. No one has taken me seriously so far. They assume I'm going to take off right back to California."

"And you're not?"

"I..."

"You probably have a good job out there. And you said yourself you never wanted to live in Crystal Cove forever."

"I have a lot to sort out." I wasn't ready to talk about the job layoff and the crushing emotions surrounding it. How I'd lost what I'd worked so long toward simply because I didn't fit the data points in the company merger. Plenty of people were laid off every day and found new jobs. I couldn't put into words why this setback stalled my momentum so hard. And how confusing it felt being home again with people who knew every little thing about me; both frustrating and a comfort. "I meant with us being together they'll see I have more than half a foot planted back in Crystal Cove."

"Do you?"

"Do I what?"

"Have more than half a—like, a full foot—" He shook his head. "Do you think you'll move back?"

"I, well... I might. I could." My breath came out in a puff in the cold air. "I have an equal shot at this house and it's too good an opportunity to pass up. We can say we've been chatting long distance and after seeing each other this weekend..." I flitted a hand in the air.

Ethan mimicked my hand motion. "Seeing each other what?"

He was going to make me say it. With actual words.

I couldn't admit the whole, embarrassing truth. That once upon a time, I'd crushed on Ethan. I'd crushed hard. Around seventh grade, it was as if a switch had turned and I became hyper aware of every interaction between us. He wasn't simply Ethan, the boy next door. He was a *boy who'd been in my bedroom.*

Ethan had scored his driver's license before most of our grade. He drove his uncle's old truck like he'd been driving since he was twelve. Driving just made guys cooler: fact. I'd seen how other girls looked at him. I became terrified he'd notice I was looking too. What if I'd told Ethan I liked him as possibly more than a friend and he cut me off for good? Never talked to me again? Better not to risk it.

By then, I'd grown into such a funk about holidays, I'd started distancing myself from my family and, by default, Ethan. I'd hated how everyone in town looked at me with sad, pitying eyes. I couldn't escape the reputation of being the kid whose parents died in a tragic accident. That sort of thing wore on a gal. I couldn't bear dumping all my humbuggery on someone so genuinely festive. Ethan had always had a heart for festive things.

Instead, I'd embraced what everyone thought of me anyway. I started wearing a lot of black. Not always black—sometimes I mixed in gray tones. I avoided anything near to or involving the word *festival.*

I found my own group of morose outcasts: theater kids (but not musical theater—too perky), science kids and brainiacs, and the public library's local anime club.

I never wanted to wreck Ethan's joy with my offbeat brand of not-actual-sadness. I wasn't sad, but everyone seemed to want me to be. I wore their expectations like I wore my family name: at times begrudgingly, but always inevitably.

All my protectiveness over Ethan and I'd ended up disengaging completely, losing the friendship anyway.

Now? None of that mattered. Dating each other made a great excuse for us to each get what we wanted. Faking the dating part, obviously.

And no way would I tell him about my crushing teenage heart. Nope. Not a chance.

I needed to spell out what I meant. I looked at Ethan. "That seeing each other the other night confirmed our...feelings. Between us. And now we're dating. Because feelings." There. I said it. "We do this for now to get what we want. Work together for the competition. I win the house, you get your land. Everybody wins." It was so simple!

"Okay." He swallowed. "I guess this is my fault since I brought up teaming together in the first place."

Fault? Yikes. "I'm not *that* much a humbug, am I? Can you stand to be around me for the season?"

"Marlowe, come on. You know that's not what I meant." Ethan's gaze lingered, as if he wanted to say more. Only he didn't. He opened the door to his truck. Not the old truck he had in high school, but one that still made him look downright hot, if I was bold enough to admit it.

Not out loud. I'd never admit it out loud.

He started the truck and rolled the window down halfway. A jingly pop song drifted out with lyrics about snow and presents under the tree.

"Ugh, holiday radio?" I waved off the putrid stench.

"Oh yeah. WKCC is twenty-four-seven holiday music. Get ready to get jolly."

Exactly what I'd asked for, and yet I dreaded the very thought of it.

I needed to make some choices.

If I aimed to stay in Crystal Cove for this ludicrous competition, I needed a plan. The next day, I texted my roommate Anna in San Jose about my plans. I scheduled my portion of the rent with automatic bill pay. I'd be good for another month rent-wise before I had to make Really Big Choices.

She texted back immediately.

Anna: *Can I call you? I have news!*

News? I sure had news too with this wacky house caper and a fake boyfriend to boot.

I responded: *Okay, call now.*

My phone vibrated in my hand. I hit answer and laid down on the bed in my old bedroom. "I hope your news isn't mouse related. I swear I patched the gap in the wall by the dryer hose—"

"Marlowe, I'm engaged! He proposed on Thanksgiving. With his whole family there!"

Not a mouse. A ring. An engagement ring. "Wow. Anna, that's amazing." Obvious shock came across in my voice. But this *was* great news. Her boyfriend, Zach, was funny, energetic, and he treated Anna like a queen. "Congratulations!"

She gave me the play-by-play, how Zach had planned with her family and his own to surprise her. The ring had been baked into some family favorite bakery's cinnamon rolls, which they ate every year on Thanksgiving morning while watching the Macy's parade on TV.

A holiday-related engagement. It almost sounded tolerable.

"That's so sweet." I hoped she understood my excitement wasn't clouded by my typical holiday grouchiness.

Anna and I met in graduate school and had been roommates for three years. She was my closest friend and the only person in my post-Crystal Cove life who knew much about my family. She and Zach started dating around this time last year. Often, the three of us hung out together for movie nights or to explore new restaurants. I'd learned to give them space in recent months. To fill my time, I'd signed up for personal training sessions at the gym and stayed late at work. I'd dated a little, but never got anywhere close to what Anna and Zach had together.

"Which leads me to something we need to figure out," Anna continued.

"Like which shade of mauve you'll pick for bridesmaid dresses?"

She snickered. She hated mauve. The word and the color. "Um, actually it's a little more important." She hesitated. "It's about our lease. It's up for renewal in February, but for changes, they require two months' notice."

"Oh, right. Sure." Suddenly, her hesitance made sense. "Two months' notice—you don't want to renew."

"Zach's family were like, *grilling* us with questions after I said yes to the proposal. His brother pointed out the cost of breaking a lease if we signed another year. We want a summer wedding—it's going to be at Zach's grandparents' farm! Then his sister offered for me to stay with her because she's looking for a roommate anyway. We can live together until the wedding."

Reality sank in. Anna needed to move out to get the next phase of her life going. If we ended our lease, I'd need to find a new place solo. An affordable place. Or a new roommate.

Along with a new job. And renewed purpose.

No job, no roommate, and the crushing sensation my quest to reinvent myself in California was about to become harder than ever.

The push to win a reality show-worthy competition for the prize of a Victorian house in the wilds of (nearly) rural Illinois became a bit more urgent. It appeared Really Big Choices had their own timeline and that time to decide was now.

"I'm sorry to spring this on you," Anna went on.

I shook my head, though she clearly couldn't see me. "No, this is fine. I mean, great. Anna, I'm so happy for you. Don't worry about me. I'll figure out what to do."

"It sounds like you have some extra time with your family. Maybe being around them will help?"

She'd been at a loss how to console me after the layoff. It seemed logical: simply apply for a new job and move on. Companies cut staff all the time; you couldn't take it personally.

I'd taken it personally. Going from a high-achieving college student to a high-achieving grad student, with no excess sad deceased parent narrative to weigh me down, I'd been unstoppable. A dependable employee since I was willing to work the holidays everyone else re-quested off. Nobody asked too many questions when you worked those holidays without complaint.

Anna and I chatted a few more minutes before she had to leave for another family function.

We ended the call and I faced the silence and fading wallpaper. This beloved house held so many conflicting memories. Despite what the town projected onto me, I'd had a happy childhood. I just loathed how my family name defined me above everything else.

If I won the house, I'd have an earned place to live. Well, sort of. I'd always known I could come back and live with Grans if needed. But coming home, to me, spelled failure. That I couldn't hack it on my own. That I couldn't survive without my family.

If I won the house, I could set my own terms. The property would be mine with no guilt of taking up space in someone else's domain.

But then I'd be in Crystal Cove, the town I'd been so desperate to escape. Still with no job and no larger purpose.

A gust of helplessness blew through me. I felt heavy and useless.

Determined not to dissolve into a funk, I dumped out my suitcase onto my bed. Tailored pieces I wore to the office mixed with upscale sporty clothes tumbled out. Ashe was right. These clothes would make me look like a snob here.

But these were the clothes I had. Not as much black and gray as the old days—I lived in somewhat sunny Bay Area California after all. But the clothes still felt out of place laid against the vintage patchwork quilt on my old iron daybed.

"This is where my lives combine," I said to the clothes pile.

The clothes didn't offer any commentary, so I went downstairs to tell Grans the good news. I was staying. I wouldn't give her an end date. Even holiday magic couldn't come up with that.

Chapter 6

Marlowe

Once I told Grans I intended to stay through Christmas—to which she nearly wept (nearly, because Grans had tear ducts of steel, unless the situation involved puppies or newborn babies)—she offered use of Gramps' old car. Gramps passed on while I was in college as an undergrad. His car hadn't been close to new then, so this would be interesting.

I returned Godzilla's Mama to the nearest rental car facility, with an assist from Shawn driving Grans' car to bring me back to the house. Now I had my own free ride. Murdoch, a cushy luxury town car that had been the height of elderly affluence in the decade when it was still manufactured. Gramps named the car after a guy he befriended on a tropical cruise. The inside of the car was spotless. Rich, burgundy velvet with leather accents. It smelled faintly of apple and old playing cards.

Murdoch was a boat compared to my compact Honda in San Jose. Driving this car reminded me of being carted around town before I had my own driver's license. When I'd filled the back seat with book hauls from the library. Or with friends on the way to the local two-screen movie theater in town.

Today, the tree lighting in town would kick off Grans' grand games or whatever. Now committed to this thing, it was time to get rolling.

Ashe and Cara arrived at the house to coordinate carpooling into town. The drive wasn't far, but this was standard practice among the family. Gather in one location and subsequently argue about who rode in whose car.

"Can we ride with you?" Mallory, their middle kid, bounced toward me. The girl literally traveled by bouncing.

I glanced to Ashe. He shrugged. "Fine with me."

Tyler, their oldest and a middle schooler, sauntered over. He looked like a mini Ashe without the broad shoulders. "I'll go with you."

A wash of emotion hit. I'd hang onto that cool auntie vibe for as long as it lasted. "I'm taking Murdoch, so pile in."

"Might as well take them all." Cara steered their youngest, Adam, toward me. "Have at it."

The kids chattered during our uneventful drive into town. Downtown Crystal Cove bustled with joyful looking people. Adults wearing big wide grins and children pointing and exclaiming. A decidedly festive quality permeated the air.

I involuntarily cringed.

I parked Murdoch and began deep breathing. What was the yoga mantra Anna used to say? *Om* something?

"You okay, Auntie Mar-Mar?" my youngest nephew Adam asked. I'd cringe at the nickname if it didn't sound so darned cute coming out of his squeaky little mouth. Honestly, I was relieved he'd refrained from barking.

"Yup. Everything is *perfect.*"

He for sure didn't believe me—or care. I herded him and his two older siblings toward the town square to meet the rest of the family. We found them convened by a row of temporary little shops bordering the square. Ah, the Holiday Haus markets. I snapped a selfie for proof of my full participation. Could I leave now?

Grans strode toward us and I swore the growing crowds parted for her. "Is everyone here and accounted for? I'd like to get the Holly Games started."

"I thought it was The Great Holly House Caper," my cousin Riley said.

The Grande dame herself scrunched her nose. "The Holly Games sounds more modern. Like that teen movie Marlowe used to like."

I coughed. "That was about children forced to kill—"

"It's not literal," Grans said quickly.

Ethan arrived, just in time for my sanity. Seeing him instantly eased my urge to bolt. He smiled easily, like none of this stressed him at all.

Okay, I could do this. *We* could do this.

"What did I miss?" he asked.

I unclenched my teeth. "There's still time to back out." As much as I needed him, he deserved the offer.

"No way. I love Holly Days. This will be fun."

He moved closer to me, probably to stay off the sidewalk. I found myself inching nearer to him. Ethan was the kind of guy comfortable in a crowd, and not lost in one. He always seemed to know where to go and what to do. When it came to Crystal Cove, I'd willfully turned off those instincts. I could manage just fine on my own elsewhere. I needed to get over this reaction to being home. Enjoy this time for what it offered—time with my nieces and nephews, my siblings and cousins. Time with Ethan.

Grans urged a group of people into our already-healthy mass. "Let me introduce you to our judges. Members of the book club and historical society. And of course, Tammy Leigh."

A teenager with dyed black hair in a pink puffer coat and rocking the smoky eye look lifted a hand in a detached greeting. "I go by TL now."

Beside me, Uncle Joe swore. Aunt Sunny swatted him. "Be nice."

"Our kids deserve the house," he grumbled. "Shouldn't be up to some teenager to decide."

Uncle Joe had a point, and for once, he made his point without a speech involving a long past war. But I deserved the house as much as his kids. Time to get serious here.

Time to get...*festive*.

Grans finished introducing her judges and continued. "Today, before dusk settles and the tree lights come up, I have the most fun activity for you. A scavenger hunt. Through town!"

Her delight would have been contagious if I wasn't already inoculated against holidays.

The kids squealed and jumped around.

"Tammy—er, TL, can you please hand out the worksheets?" Grans instructed.

My heart seized at the sight of a list on honest-to-goodness holiday-themed printer paper. While I thoroughly detested its very existence, the whole idea *was* incredibly thoughtful. Grans wanted us working together. Festively.

"Who's keeping time?" Ashe asked.

An elderly hand raised from a member of the historical society.

Ashe held up his wrist. "Is your watch set to the official government clock?"

"The government has a clock?" his daughter asked. "Is it in a tower like Big Ben?"

"Are the kids helping?" Shawn asked with a clear note of annoyance. "If so, unfair advantage."

Besides Ashe and Cara's three kids, we had Riley's daughter Reece, then Rafe and Brianne's two kids, who all spanned upper elementary ages. Brianne apparently wasn't present today, having claimed she had a school fundraiser to check up on. Over a holiday weekend? A true PTA queen. Was it too late to ditch this gig and join her?

"You may select who you'd like for your team." Grans took in the scene. "The children can be divided among the teams as helpers."

A barrage of noise erupted from the kids, who insisted they determine which teams they belonged to. Ethan and I were the lucky recipients of Mallory and Adam. Tyler went with Shawn. Riley's daughter, Reece, had volunteered to be on my team, but Rafe hauled her back.

Okayyy. So much for family bonding.

Riley and Rafe exchanged heated words I couldn't make out. Rafe looked at me with a calculating expression, then back to Riley. He pointed to their list. Riley nodded and they drew their collective three kids in closer.

Teaming up with each other, apparently. Talk about unfair. Weren't they competing against each other? None of the judges remarked on the pairing.

I tugged Ethan's sleeve to tell him about the total unfairness when Grans cut in. "Ready, set, Holly!" she announced to groans from all the adults.

Check that, the groans came from me.

Ethan clucked his tongue. "This way. I already know where the first location is."

"Did you just cluck at me?"

"Would you prefer I whistle?"

I glared. He grinned.

I checked whether the two kids followed. "Do the scavenger stops need to be done in order? Do we need a basket? I saw Cara with a basket."

Mallory tugged at my sleeve. "Is Ethan your boyfriend, Auntie Marlowe?"

Shoot. We hadn't been holding hands or anything. Maybe it was a kid thing to ask. No, wait. We were *supposed* to be dating. But were we dating to the point where Ethan was my boyfriend? Had it gone from casual to formal already?

"Sure am," Ethan responded. "Right?" He looked at me.

"Yes." I didn't sound as confident as I had last night when I'd suggested we roll with the idea.

Mallory swung her arms in lazy circles. "Okay."

Excellent. Kids were so easy.

"Can we get hot chocolate?" she asked.

"No," I said, as Ethan answered, "After we find the first clue."

Ethan's cheeks reddened. "Sorry. I figured it could be a nice reward for solving the first riddle."

"It's a *riddle*?" I felt actual pain at this detail.

Adam danced around me wildly. "Woof? Woof woof!"

Ah. The barking had resumed.

We completed the scavenger hunt and returned to the designated spot ahead of all the other teams.

"*Yes*." I held up my hand to high-five the kids, then Ethan. "Nice work, team."

From the shadows, a slow-clapping Shawn emerged. "Nice try, Mar-Mar. But you got beat. By me."

Given he had Ashe and Cara's oldest kid, Tyler, he hadn't been slowed down by hot chocolate, a bathroom break, and a child who believed he was a dog. Every single fire hydrant...

Rafe, Riley and crew torpedoed at us in full force. Many complaints arose from realizing they were not first place. Or second.

After another ten minutes, Cara and Ashe wandered over. They held hands and looked all goo-goo eyed at each other.

"They managed to offload their kids for the hunt," Ethan noted.

Ashe grinned. "We found our fun."

"Ew." Too far.

Ashe rolled his eyes. "You're such a child."

Inside, I stewed. He'd only ever think of me as his little kid sister. I might as well have been in pigtails and diapers.

"We should probably play up the dating angle," Ethan whispered to me. "We're still acting like friends."

I snapped out of my funk. Ethan's breath tickled my ear, sending a welcome shiver across my skin. I grabbed his hand, glove to glove. I wished we could ditch the fabric barrier to feel his fingers against mine.

You know, because his hand might be warm. "Is anyone noticing we're holding hands?" I whispered back.

Ethan scanned the crowd. "No. But kids dish details and Mallory and Adam were with us for the last hour and a half. Ashe and Cara will know soon enough."

True. And then our arrangement would cement in place. This whole fake dating situation should be easy, given it was Ethan. My family knew and loved him already.

Then again, *my family knew and loved him.* If they uncovered our dating was an act, the betrayal would cut that much deeper. Not to mention their reaction to selling him a chunk of Holly land.

Because we were going to win this thing.

The judges, now seated on benches along the inner portion of sidewalk in town square, reviewed our scavenger hunt answers and the location stamps we'd procured from various shops. Yep, Grans had gotten the town involved in her game, though they didn't know the real reason we were competing.

In fact, some of the shopkeepers slowed us down. Crystal Clean Cleaners, owned by a friend of Grans, wanted my life story since age eighteen (because she knew everything prior). The gift shop clerk questioned Ethan about the hours for the tree lot and asked after his parents.

But honestly, I enjoyed seeing my hometown through my niece and her puppy's—er, her brother's eyes. Things seemed innocent again and untainted with the distance of time. The kids insisted they narrate every aspect of downtown since I hadn't been home in forever.

Yeowch, way to hit me with guilt square in the chest. Over two years since I'd last been home, and short, sparse visits in the years prior. I hadn't considered living in California as hiding from my family. I'd just been busy. Really, really busy.

Not avoiding. *Busy.*

Grans requested a photo of everyone. Corralling the group took effort. Grans being the worst offender as she kept dipping out of the frame to wave at people or give instructions to the picture takers.

Streetlamps flicked on around town square. We still had time to kill before the big tree hogged all the attention, so Ethan and I left in search of food, with strict orders to report back by Grans' appointed time.

"Thanks for being such a sport," I told Ethan. "What about your job? Don't you have to sell Christmas trees?"

"Rob's covering tonight at the farm. We have hired help at the other lot."

"Maybe I'll get bonus points for picking up a tree for the house. You got any good ones?"

He patted his chest. "The best. Just call me the Tree Daddy."

I snorted. "I will *not*."

"Hey. It's actually tough to gauge the right tree size for the space. People go too big or too small. It's a practiced art."

"I'm not calling you daddy."

"I said *Tree Daddy*."

Our walk ended at a line of food trucks at the cross street bordering the square. Barriers closed off the street to traffic with an array of picnic tables stationed across from the trucks. We bought BBQ and gourmet grilled cheeses and stuffed our faces. No regrets.

At least six people stopped to say hello. Most talked directly to Ethan, but a few recognized me, including my fourth-grade teacher and one of Grans' friends from her Jazzercize days.

After the last friendly chatterer, I had to say something. "You know *everybody*."

"That's small-town life for you." He took my trash along with his and tossed it in a nearby bin. "If you get the house, does that mean you'll live in it?"

Great question. Pertinent. Essential. I hopped up from the picnic table, freeing it for a family of five and walked beside Ethan away from the crowd. "I dunno." I winced at my own answer. "Sorry. All this came at me fast. I don't know yet. I haven't told my family this, but...I lost my job."

He slowed his pace. "I'm sorry. What happened?"

I blew out a light breath. "Layoffs. Your standard-issue, time to cut ten percent of the work force after the merger they promised wouldn't lead to job cuts. Never mind I had excellent performance ratings and worked overtime without being asked. It meant nothing to them. You know what they said to me?" My heartbeat increased revisiting the experience. "*You're young. You'll bounce back.*"

Ethan visibly winced. "I'm sorry. Do you...have anyone in California?"

"My roommate, Anna. She's a keeper."

He remained quiet.

I filled in the blanks. "I don't have anyone else. Like, a boyfriend, if that's what you're asking. I worked too much to have time for much more." I tried to make light of it, but who was I kidding? "I actually went to career seminars on weekends. I did meet-up groups to learn about corporate networking. Pretty pathetic."

"How can they cut someone who spent so much time trying to be a good employee?" He shook his head. "That's why I like working with my hands. It seems easier to see work needing to be done and do it."

"You said you wrote a business plan."

"And I've sat on it. Sometimes I wonder why I'm even trying to save the tree farm."

"What do you mean? It's the family business. Obviously, you want to save it."

Only he didn't look so sure. Or maybe the pressure to save it weighed on him. Or maybe he was tired from running around town solving holiday-themed riddles.

"I imagine there's some truth to what they said, hard as it was to hear. That you'll bounce back. You have a degree from a good school. Work experience. So much time spent learning to, what did you say? Network? That has to count for something."

I wanted to agree. A quick refresh of my resume meant I'd be ready to hit the job sites. Most people my age didn't stay at companies for more than a couple years. Totally normal. But something had felt off for a while now. When I lost the job, that *off* sense grew from a feeling to a nearly audible voice. A familiar voice I'd long ago buried, shouting to be heard again.

Now with Anna moving forward in a new direction, I needed to get my act together. Win a house and parcel out some acres like an old timey land baron.

Beside me, Ethan looked out at the growing crowd, seemingly at peace. He didn't ask more questions, but I suspected it wasn't because he didn't want to. Ethan listened. If I wasn't ready to talk, he waited. Just like he always had.

"Even though I dreaded coming back, a part of me wanted to. Desperately." The words came slowly, but they'd been lurking below the surface. I just hadn't known who to say them to. "The longer I stayed in California, the easier it became to leave my past behind. No one looked at me and instantly knew my life story. I liked that. But sometimes it's lonely. Really lonely."

A gloved hand found mine. Gently squeezed and let go.

"I kept telling myself I was doing everything I could to get my life in order," I said. "But this sadness, this *something*, kept tugging at me. I couldn't tell if the feeling was missing my family and the comforts of home or weakness that I couldn't hack it on my own."

I usually went with weakness, then doubled-down on life-improving tactics. Being the youngest in my family still ruled many of my decisions—grow up fast, prove my worth. After everything our family had been through, I owed it to my grandparents to make something of myself. They'd never asked to raise a second generation of kids, and certainly never complained. In my mind, not disappointing them meant to succeed in the big wide world outside of our small town.

A voice boomed over a loudspeaker in the town square. "T-minus fifteen minutes until tree lighting."

People around us cheered and clapped.

He caught my eye and laughed.

"What?"

"You. That look. You're, like, disgusted."

I hadn't realized I'd been making a face until he'd noticed it.

"The tree lighting is a big deal." Ethan tipped his head toward a group of adults and kids wearing plastic glasses with framed lenses in the shape of Christmas trees. "Tourists come here to see this."

They sure did. "Anyway, thanks for listening to me."

He leaned so his arm pressed against mine. "More important-ly—thanks for talking to me. I know you don't trust that kind of talk with many people."

I smiled. *That kind of talk* I reserved for Anna. She knew about my parents and how I resisted being typecast by my last name alone, but the thoughts I couldn't fully express remained murky at the bottom of my emotional seafloor. The only thing I detested more than holiday excess was the thought of being lost at sea on a flimsy raft or that floating door Rose clung to in *Titanic*. I did *not* want to go down to that murky seafloor.

There was always therapy, which I'd ventured into a couple times here and there as an adult. Experienced plenty of it as a kid. People would listen if you paid them. Lucky for me, I had at least one person here in town who listened for free.

Chapter 7

Ethan

I picked up Marlowe at the house the next day for our volunteer time. She slid into the passenger seat, and I swore we were sixteen again on the way to a house party.

Okay, that happened once. But I hadn't forgotten. As kids, we'd carpooled to school events, but by high school, Marlowe spent her time with different friends. It was like she could hardly stand being around me then. A bad combo since I'd been desperate for any shred of attention from her.

"Ugh, this song." She made a retching sound.

"I warned you the holiday station would be on."

So much for the magic of the tree lighting last night. I thought she'd turned a corner with the whole yucking on the holidays thing.

Last night had been a great moment. When the lights blinked awake on the massive tree in the town square, the crowd gasped and cheered. Beside me, Marlowe fell quiet. A colorful glow illuminated her face, revealing an expression I hadn't seen on her in years: awe.

She *liked* that big lit-up tree. I freaking knew it down to my green and red plaid socks.

But I had to play a light hand. After hearing she'd been lonely and struggling, I had a side quest for our mission together.

I wanted Marlowe to love Christmas again.

She had a legitimate reason not to like the holidays after losing her parents a few days before Christmas. Living in a town that obsessed over winter holidays carved a deep groove for her hurt to live in. I wished I'd noticed back then. No, I'd noticed. I wished I'd had the maturity to talk to her about it. I was young and didn't understand how to talk about stuff.

I barely did now.

We headed to the next town over to the county social services building. I turned into the parking lot. Your standard boring administration building.

I parked and we crossed the lot to the entrance. "How is your grandmother planning to score volunteering for the contest?"

"We have to do a report out," Marlowe answered.

I stopped walking. "A what?"

"A report out. Like a presentation." She pursed her lips and made a funny face. "I guess the book club will grade our reports or something. I don't know. I'll probably throw together a digital slide show."

Families, man. My folks were happy if I showed up on time wearing a clean shirt. Bonus if I took out the trash.

A small group waited in the front lobby. After a few minutes, a woman with a lanyard and ID badge introduced herself. We'd had to sign waivers and review a set of rules before registering. She went over all that again, followed by a building tour.

Marlowe fidgeted, looking every direction with wide eyes. She hung back as the group entered the main activities room.

"You okay?" I asked her quietly.

"I've been here before." She swallowed. "I'm almost positive this is where I saw a children's counselor. You know. After."

Oh. Oh *whoa*. Marlowe had been a toddler when her parents died in the car accident. What kind of counseling did they do with toddlers? And how would she even remember?

"Do you want to leave?" I placed my hand at her back without thinking.

She startled at first, then relaxed into my touch. She looked up at me. "No. It's weird recognizing this place. The last time I would have been here I was eight or nine. I remember this hall and this room. Group activities with other kids. Sometimes it was only me with the counselor. Other times, with my brothers or my grandparents and the counselor." She waved a hand in the air. "I'm fine. Let's catch up with the group."

I could hardly focus. I hadn't thought about Marlowe's tragedy in so long. It wasn't the first thing that came to mind when I thought of her or the Holly family. Maybe because I'd made so many other memories with them.

"The concept of this center," the staff guide continued, "is to give parents a break while we provide structured, appropriate activities for the children's needs and age ranges. As you can see, space is tight since most of the building is office space. Our other branch had to close due to budget cuts. We make it work."

Several volunteers asked questions. Marlowe hung onto every word.

After questions were answered, the guide gave us a rundown of the day. "We don't have any kids here this weekend since it's a holiday, so today you all will be helping with projects. We have a smaller therapy room we need painted. Donations to sort through, cleaning, boxes to break down."

I immediately volunteered for painting. I could paint a wall in my sleep. I even did ceilings. Shoot. I should have asked Marlowe what she wanted. This couple thing was new to me.

"Go on," she said, before I could ask. "I'll go through donations."

We divided into smaller groups to tackle projects, meaning Marlowe and I spent most of the afternoon apart. A woman and her teen son were my painting partners, making quick work of the task.

As the afternoon closed out, I hauled out trash (another specialty) and cleaned up after the work we'd done. I finished before Marlowe, who told me she'd be out in a few.

I hung out in the parking lot and checked for texts. None waited for me. Rob must have had things under control at the tree lot, or at least so he assumed. Rob didn't always ask for help when he needed it.

Marlowe walked out with one of the administrators. They hugged, said goodbye, and Marlowe returned to my truck.

She held a folder and some papers. She beamed with a smile that hit me full in the chest. "I'm signing up as a regular volunteer. So long as I pass the background check. After all, I'm going to need to fill my free time until Christmas."

"Hey, that's great. You're still, uh, okay, considering..." Man, I was bad at this.

"Yeah. I'm good. Being here threw me for a loop, but I have good memories of this place. They're just sort of scattered. I mostly remember my therapist in Crystal Cove, the one I saw through high school." She cast me a curious look. "Did I ever mention coming here when we were younger? I think I called it play group."

It came back to me. "Yeah. You did call it that. I remember feeling jealous you had some special group to play games with. Didn't I ask to go with you?"

"I don't remember. I probably would have let you. Maybe Grans stepped in. Even if she had, she wouldn't have wanted to call attention to it." A cloudy look crossed her features. "Not that it mattered. Everyone knew."

Everyone knew about the tragedy, but they didn't need to know all the family's business. I sure hadn't. Then again, I'd been a kid. All I'd cared about was running around with the Hollys, playing video games, and tearing across country roads on our bikes. The good stuff.

"You told your family yet about your job?" I asked.

She looked past me. "It's cold out here. Let me in the truck."

Okay, moving on. I unlocked the truck and she hopped inside.

She burrowed into her coat. "I told Ashe I'm working remotely. I don't know why it's so hard to admit to them I failed."

I hit High on the heat to warm her up. "You didn't fail. Whoever let you go is an idiot."

"Thanks, but I still failed. I couldn't keep a job despite the overtime I'd invested. Despite my education. I guess I wasn't worth keeping." She laughed, cold and flippant.

You're absolutely worth keeping. I couldn't say it out loud without coming off, I don't know, too into her. Screw it, it was true. "You're worth it," I stammered.

She stopped breathing. Or maybe I did. The atmosphere in the truck cab shifted like the air pressure before a storm. Thick, heavy, different.

She adjusted in her seat. "Regardless, I'm even more determined to win the house. Turns out, my roommate got engaged and plans to end our lease, so I'll also be out of a place to live."

Whoa. Well, that was big. No job, no place to live. So, she'd be coming back here, right? Was it too much to hope she'd move home?

Was it even fair that I wanted her to? Purely selfish on my part. If she moved back to Crystal Cove then, well, maybe this whole dating thing wouldn't be for pretend.

My heart raced. No, I couldn't get ahead of myself. Even if Marlowe came back, won the house, and our tree farm expanded, it didn't mean anything would change with us. Only that we'd potentially be neighbors again, with a few acres and a farm of growing trees separating us.

"In case you hadn't guessed," she went on, "I haven't told my family about the apartment lease ending."

If she told them about the job and the apartment, wouldn't her quest to inherit the house be equally as valid as us pretending to date?

I suspected she didn't see it that way. Marlowe had a whole different way of looking at life I didn't fully understand.

I was a simple guy. I liked simple.

And I liked our pretend dating arrangement. It meant more time with Marlowe to catch up on the years we'd missed. If that was how she wanted to play this, I'd play too.

I lowered the heat to a non-blasting level and tapped on the radio. A bubbly song about tinsel on a tree blared and I hit the off button. The mood didn't feel right.

As I drove, Marlowe watched the scenery out the window.

A feeling hit, a familiar one I hadn't experienced in a long time. You'd think we'd feel closer, given we were supposed to be dating. But I couldn't escape the sense I might lose Marlowe all over again.

Chapter 8

Marlowe

We had a week before the next judged holiday activity—the bake sale. I had work to do. Item number one: learn to bake.

Yikes.

Thankfully, I could escape that unwelcome task and prepare my volunteer day report instead. The family would present Friday after dinner at the house, hosted by Grans, with all the judges present.

My report required more research on the respite services. Data. I wanted all of it. I looked at publicly available reports first, digging into county budgets. I enjoyed finding patterns in data and examining projections of that data.

I expanded my search to news articles. I found a pattern of a gradual loss of funding for the respite center. Attempts at new programming led to pivoting a year later after new, underfunded programs fell through. At the same time, their service area widened, with more and more families requesting help.

I noticed an article on a pharmaceutical factory and its expansion into a larger business park in Rockford, the nearest larger town to Crystal Cove. A huge multi-million-dollar project the article predicted would bring in new jobs and tax revenue to surrounding areas. I couldn't get the image of the old, worn toys and humble activity space at the social services building out of my mind. How one industry seemed to be made of money, and the other struggled to meet even basic needs.

Something about it all itched at me, but I didn't know what to do with any of it. It just made me feel uneasy.

I spent a few hours organizing my presentation into a slideshow with a planned script I added to note cards found in my old desk. Come to think of it, I had a lot of old stuff to sort through in this room. With Grans moving out soon, I'd have to clear out my bedroom anyway.

A perfect distraction to put off baking for another day or possibly forever.

I got to work sorting and tossing. Out went old school notes and folders, childhood toys that survived past donation rounds, and abandoned clothes from high school. I filled several boxes and large plastic bags with items to donate.

My bookshelf was another story. I planned to keep all my old books. After all, they still sparked joy, and according to organization expert Marie Kondo, you were supposed to keep what made you feel joy. Useless Christmas decorations? Not so much. Old picture books and a paperback series about a group of tweens and their show ponies? *Yes, please.*

A wooden birdhouse served as a bookend against my fantasy novels. One of Ethan's 4-H craft creations. I removed it from the shelf. On the back, he'd carved his initials into the wood along with the year he'd made it. Another keeper I'd hang onto.

The following day, reality hit. I needed to get cracking on this bake sale or I'd never have a chance at winning. Ethan was counting on me to expand his family tree farm.

Ethan, who knew how to bake.

I texted him.

Me: *You made a pumpkin pie. I need to learn your ways. Any free time this week?*

Ethan: *What are you up to now? I'm at the tree farm. Come on over.*

The tree farm? I needed a kitchen and baking supplies. Cookbooks. Aprons and mixers, probably. Ah, but Ethan had a job and a life besides me. I'd have to meet him where he was. Literally.

At a freaking Christmas tree farm. With holiday music and festive shoppers. Hopefully, a weekday morning meant low tide for tree shoppers.

I ventured to the farm. Murdoch, the town car, pointed me the right direction, due north, like the famous star. Well, more like northeast, but whatever. Down the road and around the corner.

More cars than I expected filled the front lot of Sawyer's Tree Farm. How many people could possibly be buying a Christmas tree on a weekday morning?

Turned out, many. I parked a ways out to avoid clogging up the good spots. The farm extended beyond the front area set up for buyers. A charming, rustic sign displayed the Sawyer family name.

For some reason, I expected to see Ethan at the gate waiting for me. I definitely needed to get over myself. Ethan wasn't waiting around to teach me a basic life skill. I could feed myself, sure, but baking anything more than box brownies was beyond me.

"Is that Marlowe Holly?" a deep voice questioned.

"Mr. Sawyer." The sight of Ethan's dad made me smile on instinct. His round, ruddy cheeks and salt-and-pepper beard gave him a young Santa vibe.

Not that I was into Santa vibes. Just, well, the man was jolly. Facts stated.

He lifted a plaid flannel arm to pat me on the back. "Good to see you. I assume you're here for Ethan."

"Only if he's not busy." With the shoppers milling around and loud machinery noises coming from the nearby barn, my baking lesson seemed even less important. "I can always text him later."

Ethan buzzed by, giving me a head nod. "Let me take care of a thing and I'll be right there."

He wore a navy blue work coat with a gray sweatshirt hood peeking out. His skin had a natural flush from the cold. He seemed at ease. Happy. Like he existed in his element.

"We run another lot out by the highway," Mr. Sawyer told me. "Rob is there today training a seasonal hire. We sell a lot of trees there, but some folks still want to come to the farm. It's their family tradition. We can't seem to convince them otherwise."

"That makes sense. Grans gets her tree from you. Does she come out to the farm for it?"

Light danced in his eyes. "Ethan delivers one to her every year on December first."

"I didn't know you guys did delivery."

"We don't. Never asked him to do it, and I doubt your grandmother ever did either. Just something he does."

A warm sensation coursed through my chest. Something weird tickled my eyes. Suddenly a holiday song played in my head along with a filmstrip involving Ethan hoisting a freshly cut tree over his shoulder and into Hollybrooke House. A roaring fire crackled in the fireplace and warm cinnamon applesauce simmered on the stove.

Earth to Marlowe? You don't *like* that stuff, remember?

Ethan stood in front of me, clapping dirt from his work gloves. "Dad, I'm going to take a break. I'll be here for the afternoon shift."

"You don't have to—" I started.

Mr. Sawyer had already moved on while Ethan looked at me with excitement. "I've got plans for us."

"I feel like I'm intruding. I didn't know so many people would be here."

"It's okay. We hire help for the season. Come on."

I followed him to a trailer used as a business office with several rooms including a kitchen. Okay, kitchenette.

"We're going to cook *here*?" I scanned the space. Electric kettle, a microwave that had seen live combat, a weathered olive green refrigerator covered in holiday-themed magnets. Tiny scrap of counter space.

He pulled out a chair for me at a small round table. "Not here. We'll put together a battle plan. Can you bake at the house, or are your brothers and cousins still hanging around?"

We both sat. "They're at their own houses. Shawn is staying at one of those business hotels with a little kitchen. He says it's on the company dime. I wonder if it has an oven."

"Forget about Shawn. What are your family's favorite recipes? We should start there."

"I..." Drew a blank. Nothing. Zilch. "Mashed potatoes?" No. "Um, baking, right. Cookies. Sugar cookies."

Ethan tilted his head in thought. "Your grandmother has a cookbook collection. I want you to find an old and worn one and see if she's tagged any recipes."

Good idea. "How many things are we baking?"

He laid out a paper with the Holly Days schedule. Beside it, he placed the competition list Grans put together. "There's the bake sale this Saturday, so that's our focus this week. We'll need a separate plan for the Tasty Bake competition the following week."

Right. Not one but two opportunities for baking.

Ethan caught my eye. "Don't worry. I've already been thinking of ideas. I was going to text you today anyway."

I reviewed Grans' guidelines, which stated the person with the most bake sale items sold would win. For the baking competition, if any of us placed in the contest, tiers of points would be awarded, with the most points for the highest placement.

Ethan rapped a knuckle against the table. "The bake sale scoring is about quantity of items sold. The bake sale has rules, so cookies can't be individually sold, they have to be sold in lots of six or a dozen and pricing is within specific ranges for consistency. This money is going to charity, so it's not about individual profit. We need enticing products that look like a good deal when grouped together."

My head was spinning. "So sugar cookies? Those will work, right?"

"Everyone will sell sugar cookies. That's good and bad. If you don't have any, and other people sell out, it's a win if you can deliver. We'll need a mix of unique items and familiar favorites."

This sounded like a ton of work. Then again, the proceeds went to charity. Then again part two, and even more crucial, I could win the family estate.

Keep your goal front and center. Otherwise, I might puke over the obscene amount of festive activity.

"The Tasty Bake is where you want to show off." Ethan showed me a video on his phone. "You ever watch this baking competition on TV?"

"Anna does. She gets inspired and I get to eat what she bakes." I'd never regretted sampling any of her results, but I sure did regret not asking her more questions on how she'd made them.

"Excellent. Have you ever eaten one of these?" A picture of a chocolate cake in the shape of a tube with a swirl on the end stared back. Little edible holly leaves stuck out from the top.

"A neighbor used to bring us a cake like this for Grans' holiday party."

"It's a yule log cake. People love those around here. It's a promising contender if we execute it correctly."

I burst out laughing. "*Execute*? What is this, war?"

His face remained unchanged. "Do you know who runs the bake sale and judges the competition? Church ladies." He let that sit.

The church ladies ran a tight ship, er bake sale. "No further questioning, your Honor."

I flashed to memories of Grans filling up her kitchen with treats ahead of a big sale event. Grans would have me use the food scale to ensure each bundle weighed as close to the same as the others. Each item got tagged, ribboned, and labeled using a rubber stamp with her custom logo. Excellence was expected and Grans and the church ladies wouldn't allow anything less.

I'd forgotten. I'd forgotten so much. "Hold up. I don't have stamps and ribbon."

Ethan slid a hand to mine. "Your grandmother has all that stuff. Ask her for it. The ingredients we'll have to buy."

"Me—I'm buying the ingredients. This is my thing." I let out a breath. "I already feel like I'm asking you too much."

Ethan blinked at me. "You don't know how to bake, Marlowe."

"I can make brownies."

"From a box?"

It counted. "Okay. I'm just saying, I'm not entirely helpless."

"If you make a dry cake, you're out."

The fact I was about to ask what made a cake dry proved his point. "Let's save cakes for later. Bake sale first. Where should I start?"

"Go through those cookbooks and pick out recipes. Cookies, cookie bars, maybe some brownies. I'll review the options and we'll narrow to final choices. Then make an ingredient list, go to the store, and bring the stuff back to your house."

Okay, I could do this. I had project management training. "I'm going to need my laptop and some quality time with Excel."

"You need spreadsheets to make cookies?"

"You don't?"

He smirked. "Whatever works. You want to win, right?"

I did. Very much.

And of course, Ethan was aiming for his chance too. He wanted the land as much as I wanted—and possibly now needed—the house.

I'd truly forgotten so much.

Strike professional baker from my career options. One afternoon baking on my own and I needed to call in reinforcements.

The organization part I could handle. Recipe finding, inventory of baking supplies, ingredient lists. I'd found the holy grail cookbook on Grans' shelf. As soon as I pulled it down, the memories flooded back. Yellowed pages, some wrinkled and stained from where ingredients fell against the recipes, revealed a history of treats I'd eaten in childhood.

Ethan assured me he had plenty of free time around his work schedule. He showed up with extra brown sugar—how did he know?—and a relaxed, confident attitude that put me at ease.

With our first batch of sugar cookies in the oven, I grabbed a new flour bag and carefully opened it. I turned toward the stand mixer at the same time Ethan moved past me.

We collided.

Poof. Flour shot from the open sack into my face. I yelped and squeezed my eyes shut, waiting for the powder cloud to settle. I sputtered. Flour dust landed in my mouth.

I opened my eyes to Ethan mere inches from me.

"You have a little dust on your cheek." He said it with a straight face.

I blinked rapidly. "It's coating my eyelashes. This flour is worse than sand!"

Ethan only grinned and handed me a dry dish towel. "Stand over the sink and brush some of it off dry before—"

Too late, I'd already run the towel under the faucet and smacked it against my floury face. I jerked the towel away when I realized what he said.

His expression remained completely still.

"It's bad isn't it?"

Without speaking, he took the towel and dabbed the area around my eyes.

I couldn't breathe. He stood so close. He dabbed so gently.

A buzzing sounded in my head. Ethan's presence felt welcome and wanted. High school Marlowe would have incinerated with embarrassment over imagining him wiping my face with such care. Or cracked up laughing, ruining the moment.

But I didn't dare laugh. This wasn't funny. This was...sexy.

Yes, I was a hot mess with dry ingredients now wetly smeared across my face who considered this moment sexy. I had issues.

Ethan physically turned my body at the shoulders and pointed me toward the hall bathroom. "Go clean yourself up, you heathen."

The moment shattered, I scurried to the bathroom to wash up. *What was that out there?* Me going googly eyed over my high school crush? The man was trying to win land. He didn't care how his gentle dish towel caresses sent me to a romantic place.

Get a grip, lady. Ethan wasn't interested in me romantically. He never had been or he would have obviously said or done something by now. He needed the land in our deal. Simple as that.

By Friday, treats were baked and sorted in plastic containers. I had one last batch of sugar cookies in the oven so we'd have extra just in case.

So far, we'd operated professionally since the dish towel incident. If professional included constantly joking with each other and a mishap where I miscalculated measurements and added a teaspoon of celery salt to a cookie batch instead of cinnamon. Was it my fault the spice packaging all looked the same and I'd also accidentally switched the labeled lids?

Yes. Yes, it was my fault.

For bake sale packaging, I found holiday ribbon and the Holly family stamp Grans had used during her peak bake sale production days. Using Grans' stamp felt a little like cheating. Relying on the family name I'd worked so hard to separate myself from.

Ethan arrived that afternoon, causing a ruckus in the hall.

"That must be my tree." Grans swept by my cookie operation to the door.

Ethan walked past the kitchen doorway moments later hauling a huge tree through the house. I glanced at my fitness tracker watch. December first. Like Ethan's dad said—he personally delivered Grans' Christmas tree.

I'd helped Grans bring out boxes of decorations earlier. She didn't ask, but I couldn't let her do the work alone, regardless of my feelings on figurine villages and hokey decor where collecting dust was its sole purpose.

Ethan set up the tree in a stand in the exact spot it always went, in the corner of the family room by the big window. A smaller, fake tree adorned the front parlor, facing out to the street. This tree could only be seen by the family inside or by walking through the yard.

He found me in the kitchen a few minutes later. I'd retreated here after I found myself staring while he worked. He'd peeled off his flannel down to a light gray T-shirt that hugged his arms in an extremely appealing way.

"Check this out." He grabbed his coat and unearthed a wood block from the pocket. "For you."

A stamp was affixed to the block with a new logo on it. *Marlowe Holly* was spelled out in a cursive font encased by a decorative circle. Fresh and modern and mine.

I gasped. "How did you get this? And when? So fast?"

He laughed. "I've got a buddy with a 3D printer. Rob's good at design, so I had him create the logo. We've always got wood around, so the construction part was easy."

The wood had been sanded smooth and shined on the top as if a gloss seal had been added. No words came.

"If you don't want to use it, that's fine. No big—"

I threw my arms around him. A moment of pure joy filled me. Breathless, I pulled back. "It's perfect. I can't believe you had time to do this. You *made* this."

His cheeks went ruddy. It was freaking adorable. Ethan had always been shy with compliments. I'd tried to lob them his way delicately, even with trickery, so he couldn't deflect. He was a hard one to thank.

We stood there, close and breathing each other's air. Again. I felt those dish towel romantic vibes pulsing beneath my skin. Ethan *made me a custom stamp.*

My heart raced. "Thank you."

"Seriously, it's not a big deal. I got the idea from a lady who buys wood odds and ends from us. She makes stamps and sells them at craft shows. Anyway, how's the operation going? Are we ready to package?"

Awe still struck me over the small stamp with my very own logo. It was exactly what I wanted. To be distinguished apart from my family in my own unique way. Honestly, it was what I'd always been trying to do in every part of my life. Somehow a simple stamp conveyed the entirety of my life's goals.

Maybe I needed bigger goals.

"Marlowe?"

"Yeah, I'm here. Just thinking. That's been happening a lot lately."

A beat passed before he spoke again. "It's just, the oven timer went off. Whatever's in there, you don't want it to burn."

Chapter 9

Marlowe

Friday evening at the house, guests arrived for the report-out dinner.

"This is absurd," Cara was saying to Ashe in the library. The room had warped French doors which never closed the right way, so everyone left them open. "You're not a child."

"Do you want the house or not?" Ashe asked, exasperated.

"Not! How many times have I told you, we don't need this house or this contest. Play along if you feel the need, but I'm not role playing in your presentation."

Cara walked out, and I slipped in. "Trouble in *Holly*wood?" I snickered at my own joke.

Ashe stared out the window, blocking a good chunk of the waning daylight with his large, checked-print frame. "You wouldn't understand."

"Oh, here we go. The baby of the family never understands *anything*." I wandered farther into the room. Closer in, to antagonize him. "Why are you still in the game? Cara's not even on board."

"This isn't only Cara's decision," he snapped.

"I heard that!" Cara called from another room.

Ashe growled. A literal growl. "So, you're dating Sawyer, huh? Getting ready to play house with the family fortune?"

I ignored his barb. And now I knew for sure one of the kids had spilled about the dating news. Just like we expected. "Would it be so bad if I came back?"

His shoulders softened as he stepped from the window. "Of course not. The kids would love to have their cool aunt around. They ask about you."

"They do?" I sort of assumed they only cared when I sent them stuff.

"And, well, you're always welcome to visit. I hope I've made that clear."

I shrugged in response. My emotions stirred with deeper thoughts I didn't have the bandwidth to think through. I'd come in here to poke at him when he was vulnerable and now he'd turned the tables on me. What was with this freakish soft side? He must have recently become infected. Stupid holidays.

I trailed my finger against the frame of a family photo from a long-past Christmas, when Gramps had still been around. "I love this house too. I like the idea of kids being here and filling up the rooms. I wouldn't close you guys off or anything."

He raised a questioning brow. "You and the Sawyer brother thinking of tying the knot? Raising some kids?"

That escalated quickly. "We're *dating*. I've been home a week."

"But you've known him your whole life. Should've figured he'd be the one to bring you back. He's been at the house every day this week."

"Are you *spying* on me?" How did he know so much?

Ashe laughed. "Small town, Mar. I drive by the house on my way to work. Less traffic on this back road. I've seen his truck here."

If I lived here again, I'd never be free from meddling. It would be my family in my business all the time. The thing I loathed and loved at the same time.

"It's not only Ethan who brought me back. Grans summoned me. She summoned all of us."

"Yeah, but you could have blown her off. You have before."

His accusation stung. But this time, he was reacting to what I'd constructed myself—an identity apart from my family. An identity I'd spent a lot of years protecting. And for what?

Ashe turned to me, but instead of older brother vitriol, he looked tired. "I always dreamed of raising kids here, in some way. Holidays, summers, like we had. The kids used to sleep over every weekend in the summer. Now sports and friends take up Tyler and Mallory's time. Adam comes with us wherever the big kids go. It's just...different."

"Is Adam still barking?"

"Yep. He asked for his dinner to be put in a bowl on the floor."

"Committed to the bit."

"Crazy thing is, we did it. At least he ate the dinner, including the vegetables. That's a win." He sighed. "I miss the simpler days."

I leaned against a built-in bookcase. Dark-stained wood with clean lines, it looked almost modern. "Was it ever simple?"

"Yes." His eyes grew sadder. "Before."

After a tense dinner where I focused on schmoozing with the judges and ignoring my blood relations—after all, we were in competition—everyone gathered in the family room for the presentations.

Cara offered herself for dish duty and holed up in the kitchen. The rest of us sat facing the fireplace mantle serving as backdrop for the presentation stage. Across the room, the fresh scent of pine emitted from the Christmas tree Ethan brought over. I didn't mind the twinkle of the lights so much. Or the memory of watching him heft the tree into the room.

Rafe and his family went first with their presentation. They'd volunteered at a local food pantry that received most of its donations from a warehouse hub who distributed to small towns across several counties. I found myself fascinated by the statistics. I'd never gone hungry a day in my life and hadn't considered who might struggle for food in our community. I felt foolish for thinking it, but hunger seemed more like a problem for larger cities with expensive rents and higher rates of homelessness. Not close-knit communities like Crystal Cove.

Usually Rafe became eyerollingly preachy about anything he talked about, but here he came off more subdued. As if he'd learned a thing or two himself from the experience.

Riley and her daughter Reece presented on the animal shelter. By chance, they'd gotten their names in ahead of the Holly Games for the popular volunteer option. To Riley's credit, she didn't stuff a slide show with cute kitten and puppy pictures, but showed photos of the facility itself in need of a renovation. They'd painted and cleaned up a storage room. Riley and Reece had done real work and hadn't simply pet cute animals.

Shawn went next. He shuffled to the front of the room. "I, uh, wanted to do the animal shelter too cuz I figured it'd be easy. Couldn't get in, so decided to go with the rehab center. Where Gramps learned to walk again after his first stroke. Wanted to, uh, help out to, uh, give back." He coughed and wiped his eye.

My mouth hung open. This was not slick business guy Shawn. He had an honest-to-goodness tear in his eye. I knew instantly he wasn't acting. Shawn didn't act. In fact, he was so bad at acting, he'd been turned away from the middle school theater production and redirected to set design. *Middle school theater.*

This whole night surprised me. Now, my turn.

I stood and opened my laptop to present the slide show. On auto-pilot, I went through what I'd rehearsed. Facts and figures with photos of the respite facility pulled from their website.

As I wrapped up, my gaze connected with Grans. She dabbed her eye with a tissue. What was with everybody crying?

I looked at Ashe, then Shawn. It hit me all at once like it had at the respite center. We'd *all* been there. Not just me. We'd faced the worst reality—losing our parents and moving on without them, without fully understanding what that meant.

And we'd done it together.

I ditched the rest of my script. "Honestly, this experience meant a lot to me. To see the facility again as an adult with some distance put in perspective how crucial their services are. I'm looking into ways I can work with them more. While I'm here. So, thanks, Grans, for making this a part of the Holly Games. It felt really worthwhile."

I looked at Grans again. She wore a satisfied smile. I couldn't be sure if my eyes were tricking me, but she almost looked smug.

Chapter 10

Ethan

Saturday we dropped in hot to the bake sale, ready to kick butt and take names.

Okay, I was into this. Way into this.

I delivered Marlowe and our squadron of treats to the congregational church the moment its ancient doors creaked open. I nearly pushed Violet Muldron aside to be first seller in, but Marlowe had the sense to hold me back.

"Cool your jets, Ethan. We don't want to be disqualified."

"On what grounds?"

"Inciting a cookie riot? I don't know. Let the old ladies pass."

Violet Muldron paused and squinted at Marlowe over her glasses. "I heard that. Seventy-five is the new fifty-five. That's what they say on the daytime talk shows."

"Sorry, ma'am," I blurted to cover for Marlowe.

Violet turned her reprimand on me. "And don't call me ma'am. I'm seventy-five, not ninety."

As we followed the elder baker inside, she turned to Marlowe again. "Aren't you Emmaline's youngest granddaughter? Are you back home now? Never thought it wise for you to run off to Hollywood the way you did. A young girl needs her family."

"I'm twenty-six." But Violet had already moved on. "This is why—" Marlowe started and waved the rest away to the air. "Never mind."

I snickered, lowering my voice. "Naturally, you'd end up in *Holly-wood*—"

"The Bay Area is over three hundred miles from there." Her nose scrunched. "Stop provoking me."

But provoking her netted cute results. Why stop?

Carrying our loaded boxes, we headed downstairs to the church's all-purpose room where linoleum and knotty pine lived out its last days. Folding tables topped with red tablecloths lined the room in a U-shape.

"Wow, this place is a time capsule," Marlowe mused. "Look, here's our table." A little tent sign on the table noted *Holly, M.* She removed her coat and set it aside.

My jaw hit the linoleum.

Horror crossed her features. "What? What's wrong?"

I couldn't believe my eyes. "You're wearing a holiday sweater."

She sighed. "I thought you were going to say we forgot the almond tassies. We better have those almond tassies. Anyway, I found this sweater in Grans' closet. It fit."

"Brilliant." It wasn't her style at all, but it appeared well made. A knitted snowy scene with a holiday sleigh and snowflakes down the sleeves. Almost every baker coming through the doors wore a version of a holiday sweater.

I took off my own coat.

Marlowe's horror returned. "Does your clothing...light up?"

I clicked a button and the reindeer nose on my sweatshirt blinked to red. "Like it?"

"*Love* it." She mimed doubling over and hurling into a nearby trash bin.

"Whatever helps. I really want to win—er, you to win."

"This is definitely an *us* thing," she said. "I couldn't have done any of this without you."

I liked how this was an us thing. I liked it very much.

She moved to my side. "Should we have coordinated our outfits? I didn't even think of that. Like those annoying couples who wear matching shirts."

"If you're into plaid flannel and light-up reindeer sweatshirts, you're on. That's my entire wardrobe."

"It's not." She swatted me, but hung onto my arm, giving me a little extra caress.

I also liked this very much.

The room filled quickly with bakers. Marlowe's family arrived one after the other, setting up at tables around the room. I scouted the competition. Her cousin Riley and her daughter arranged a nice set-up with wooden snowman decorations they must have brought from home. Rafe and crew had brought in expensive looking glass dishware and cake stands to display their baked treats. Silver ornaments sat in clusters between the dishes. His wife Brianne paced behind the table talking on her phone while the kids sat on the floor slumped over electronic devices.

"Are these enough?" Marlowe pointed toward the fresh greens I'd nabbed from the farm. "Some of the decorations people have on their tables is way more elaborate than ours."

I opened a cookie bin and began placing the bagged items across the table. "Classic is good. People like a classic look." I hoped. "Hey, how did the presentations go?"

"They were surprisingly meaningful and informative. Annoyingly, Grans awarded everyone equal points. There was no winner. It was all a ploy to get us to contribute to the community."

"That actually makes more sense than judging volunteering. But yeah, annoying."

I already knew the respite facility had made an impact on Marlowe, so I couldn't fault her grandmother for the setup. But the bake sale would count for real points. As would the baking competition in the town square next weekend. We needed every point to get ahead.

After running between the tree farm and the highway sales lot all week, it couldn't have been more obvious we needed more land. Once we expanded the farm, we could bring on more help. The way we operated now, we couldn't justify bringing on more regular full-time staff without the larger vision and business plan.

And if selling cookies got us there, then that was what I'd do.

Marlowe and I reviewed our attack plan. I'd be man out front, greeting shoppers in the space in front of our table with our sample tray. Broken and ugly cookies that didn't pass our final cut were divided into smaller pieces for free sampling. Marlowe would handle the sales and backstock.

"Are you sure your sales approach is necessary?" Marlowe scanned the room. "Everyone else is behind their tables. Not in front."

I leaned toward her. She smelled like lavender and something else sweet I couldn't name. Probably twenty types of cookies. "That's exactly why it works. We have competition. We want buyers interested in *our* sugar cookies. Not some third-rate cut-out that for all we know could be dough from a can."

Marlowe snickered. "This side of you is compelling. I always remember you being so nice."

"I *am* nice." Just competitive. And I had a goal.

Arlene Elmhurst, a put together lady in her sixties pinned with an official staff ribbon, inspected our stock for consistency in packaging and pricing. She found no errors. Marlowe and I made a great team.

Before we knew it, the doors opened to the public and eager customers arrived wide-eyed and ready for a sugar high. The bake sale, as I'd reminded Marlowe through the week, made for big news in the community. The sale was advertised on the radio and social media.

Marlowe peered past me. "Is that Benny Arends? Working the door?"

We'd all graduated together. "Yup. There's usually a line to get in lasting the whole sale. Benny's working line management and crowd control."

Marlowe muttered something I couldn't hear. Probably not anything cheerful, which was why I was the front guy. A gaggle of gray-haired ladies headed our way. The tray came out, and I went to work.

The first round of samples disappeared in ten minutes—all leading to sales.

"Hey, what do you think you're doing?" Shawn called from across the room as an opening appeared among the crowd. He pointed at me. "You can't give away samples!"

Ah, but I could. "There's nothing in the rules stating samples are off-limits."

Shawn dug through a bag behind his table to pull out the printed rules. He could afford the distraction since no one shopped at his table.

I refilled the sample tray and went back to work. The tray, and my sales pitches, worked their magic until the tray emptied.

When a lull hit, Emmaline Holly herself appeared. She had on her own fancy holiday sweater, understated and classy, as always. "You look to be doing well." Her gaze danced between us. "I'm so pleased to hear you two are settling in."

Whew, I knew this moment was coming, but it was a doozy. Telling Shawn and Ashe's kids that Marlowe and I were dating? Sure, easy. Telling that lie to Emmaline Holly? Genuine fear.

Thankfully, she didn't expect an answer. Maybe she'd mistaken my dopey look for love, not open terror.

"Your stock looks low," Mrs. Holly commented. "We have an hour of the sale to go."

"If we sell out first in the family, do we get extra points?" Marlowe asked.

Mrs. Holly's eyes sparkled. "What a novel idea. I'll run it by TL." She took out her phone and sent a text. "TL has an orthodontist appointment that couldn't be rescheduled. Those Saturday appointments go quickly."

I really had to wonder what was in it for teen TL. She didn't seem all that interested in any of this.

Not far behind, several of Emmaline's judges gathered at our table. A middle-aged Black woman wearing gingerbread cookie-shaped earrings inspected a wrapped bundle of ...gingerbread cookies. No surprise there. "Would you look at that—Marlowe's got her own logo."

Mrs. Holly examined the bundle. "How clever."

"Ethan *made* it for the sale." Marlowe beamed my way. "Isn't he so enterprising? We offered samples of all our products until they ran out."

A white man in glasses, probably well over seventy, carried a mini flip pad and made a note with a sharp pencil. "Samples! That's neat. Your idea?"

I wasn't used to this much attention. Well, at least, when I wasn't asking for it. "I come here every year and always wished I could try the stuff before I bought it."

Ashe walked over, a hulking presence in plaid flannel. "Hey, Grans. How is everything?"

She beamed at him. "Wonderful. Let's keep moving. I want to see your table. This is so *fabulous* having all my grandkids selling items for charity."

I glanced at Marlowe who rolled her eyes. But she was smiling.

Something told me her grandmother didn't seem concerned with who won the bake sale. With all the Holly kids here in one place, I couldn't blame Emmaline Holly for liking it too.

As they moved on, Rafe's steady stare from across the room landed on me. Was he scowling? At a cookie fair?

The man was intense. And intense about winning.

As long as there was a land prize to win, I couldn't forget this was a competition.

We sold all of our bake sale stock before the others in Marlowe's family. Each of them had bundles leftover. Us? Only crumbs.

Marlowe hugged me. "We did it! What a week." She pulled back, giving me every bit of her attention.

Her family lingered nearby. We needed to keep up our act. I tugged her closer.

Her eyes widened in shock until I whispered, "We're dating, remember?"

She nodded, blushing. "What would I have done without you?" She looked up at me, her arms still anchored around my neck. I swore she meant every word.

Dangit, my heart tugged at her declaration. I'd missed that—her needing me. "You know I'd do anything to help you."

"And for the prize." She winked at me. "Obviously."

She unattached herself and began cleaning up the table. I was definitely keeping my sights on the prize. Only sometimes those sights got a little sidetracked by a Marlowe smile.

I wanted more Marlowe smiles in my life.

"Hey, so next we'll need to pick out a cake to make for Tasty Bake next week." More baking time together. Maybe she'd douse herself with flour again. Pathetically cute and surprisingly hot.

Her shoulders slumped. "More baking. Just what I want after a week of baking."

I took her stack of presentation plates and loaded them into our plastic bin. "You're practically a pro now. We won this round of the contest."

"I seriously couldn't have done it without you. It's more like you won this round."

One step closer to what we both wanted.

My mind jumped to New Year's. Would Marlowe still be here? What about January? I'd been soaking up every moment with her. Getting used to those moments.

I was setting myself up for potential disaster. Because honestly? I wanted more than land for the farm. I wanted...Marlowe.

Too late to guard my heart against it. I was already falling for Marlowe all over again.

Chapter 11

Marlowe

After the bake sale, Ethan took off to the tree farm. For the rest of the weekend, the farm would take his attention, leaving me free to do anything I wanted.

Freely. So free.

Not working left a hefty dose of empty time to fill. I ended up at Ashe and Cara's for dinner and games with the kids. Sunday, I attended church with Grans and Shawn, followed by a lazy day lounging around the house and watching TV.

Monday, I needed a real kick in the pants. A kick to the life pants. I started my own side project: aka, Girl, Get Your Life Together. I contacted the respite center to ask about volunteering. Surprisingly, they asked me to come in for an interview the same day.

I only waited a few minutes when the volunteer coordinator, a tall Black woman wearing a cable knit gray sweater, summoned me to her office. "Hello, I'm Sheree Bolden. Nice to have you back, Marlowe. Come into my office."

Bright light shone in on a plant-filled office. Greenery spilled out from crocheted hanging baskets, and succulents in tiny, colorful pots crowded the corner of her desk.

We chatted for a few minutes about what drew me to the respite center and which volunteer roles were available.

"We expect a six-month commitment up front and then re-evaluate." Sheree slid papers across the desk.

My smile froze in place. Six months. Where would I be in six months? Everything sane inside me informed me I'd be back in California, in a new apartment and working for a business happy to utilize my skills. I had no guarantee I could win Grans' house, and even then, the logistics of moving—

"Miss Holly?" Sheree looked at me with a kind, but mildly concerned expression. "The time commitment can throw some folks off. Would you like to discuss it?"

"Um..." Swallowing proved difficult. "I'm here on extended leave from my job—" Not true. I couldn't lie to a woman who planned to perform a background check. Including fingerprints running me through the law enforcement system. "Actually, sorry, I'm between jobs now. It's hard to get used to that. I don't have a plan beyond Christmas—well, see I do, but it's contingent on a few...things."

The warmth remained in her smile. This woman was a saint. "Understandable. We ask for a minimum of six months as the children often become attached to our volunteers. Having new staff cycle in and out too frequently can be hard on them. Also, the time it takes for training and oversight, it's not cost efficient for us to invest in volunteers who are more or less transient."

Transient. I was a transient. A shifty squatter with no real home. Of course they wouldn't want someone like me with no ability to commit to a volunteer role. They didn't care about a glossy graduate degree from a top-rated school. They wanted commitment. A promise.

Which I couldn't keep. I didn't know enough about my life's plan beyond these next few weeks. This was supposed to be my starting point in figuring that out.

"Is there anything I can do to help in the meantime? Anything not involving direct work with children or intensive training? Things like I did for the volunteer day?"

Sheree sat back, thoughtful. "There just might be. I'll have to run it by the staff. We've used high school interns here and there over the years. Believe me—I won't turn down free help."

Hope. Hope existed. "Thank you. I appreciate it."

I left Sheree my cell phone number and she promised to be in touch.

I'd tried. Tried and failed to fill my life with something more meaningful. Okay, a temporary failure. One setback. I returned to Murdoch and blasted the heat. I had time to kill, so how best to use it?

I left the parking lot and headed toward town with no real destination in mind. Murdoch read my thoughts and turned on the road leading to the tree farm.

The rest of the week, moving through the kitchen beside Ethan became second nature. When he wasn't needed at the tree farm, he spent his time at Hollybrooke House baking with me or doing various tasks Grans didn't directly ask of him. Each day, Ethan let himself in through the side door and we picked up the conversation as if no time had passed.

We established little routines. I liked assembling what we needed and combining the dry ingredients. Ethan thrived on the finer details on how we could set our cake apart for the Tasty Bake competition. He liked tweaking recipes whereas I stuck close to the directions aiming to get the basics right.

We'd clean up the kitchen to Grans' standards, then Ethan would take off to check on the farm. Usually, he'd end up back here for dinner.

Having Ethan around again, resurrecting old in-jokes and creating new ones, sometimes made me forget about the contest. This was the most fun I'd had in a long time.

With our latest test cake in the oven, we hung out in the kitchen talking. I caught myself looking at Ethan a beat longer than expected. Scratch that—*he* caught me.

"What?" he asked. "Dumb idea?"

"Uh, no." I couldn't remember what he'd even said. "It's fine. The cake, right?"

"I was talking about this podcast I found on woodworking. That I might do their project challenge in January." He made a face. "That's probably super boring to you, sorry."

"No, that's cool. Sorry, I zoned out." Today he had on a dark gray Henley shirt and worn but clean jeans. I found myself marveling at how mature he seemed, while still acting like the guy I'd run around with as a kid. I wanted to know everything about this familiar-but-new person I'd been spending so much time with.

He knocked once against the countertop. "I guess we should make a game day plan for Tasty Bake."

I snorted laughing. My hand flew to my mouth to stifle my cackles.

"What? Now I'm getting paranoid."

I shook my head. "It's just...Tasty Bake. To hear you act so serious about a thing called *Tasty Bake*."

"Okay, whatever." He made a show of walking off.

He sharply circled back and grabbed me so quickly I squealed. Hauling me over his shoulder, he left the kitchen and tossed me onto the big couch in the family room.

"Ethan!" I shrieked, laughing.

"You dare to laugh at Tasty Bake?" He stood over me, smirking. "I'll have you know Tasty Bake is a real challenge. One of the judges is a trained pastry chef."

My laughter petered out. He was right. This part of the competition would be more challenging than the bake sale. This involved real judges, not limited to Grans' crew. Though they'd be there too.

"I'm getting worried," I admitted as I stood again and returned to the kitchen. "Maybe I haven't taken this cake seriously."

As my recipe testing proved, I did not excel at the baking arts. My first yule log cake came out dry. The second too doughy, so not baked long enough. The rolling up process often took out chunks of my cake. I never expected to dust sugar on a dish towel as part of a recipe. I was meant to lay the cake flat against the clean and dusted towel, then to roll into a log shape. I had to get the timing right before the cake fully cooled but wasn't too hot either.

"Maybe we pivot," Ethan suggested. "The yule log is a classic, but we can do better."

We pulled out Grans' cookbooks again and went to work searching for the right recipe.

I hadn't felt this happy about cooking...probably ever. I was pretty sure it had to do more with the cook than the book.

We decided on a cake and made a new plan. Test bake first and refine from there. After the cake cooled, we experimented with decorating. Anyone who could pipe a cake with buttercream frosting deserved infinite respect.

Ethan had an early start the following morning, so I walked him out. As usual, we stood by his truck door talking for too long until I started shivering.

"Here, take my coat." He handed it over.

"No, it's fine. You're leaving. I should wear my own coat out. This happens every time."

His grin turned my insides to pudding. Probably figgy pudding since my life had turned so darned festive these days.

I slid on the coat and burrowed down. The lingering warmth from his body paired with faint woodsy tree scents provided instant comfort. A quiet hush descended between us. The dark sky offered the perfect backdrop for stars. With the perfect companion for stargazing.

"Remember when we used to look at the stars?"

He grinned. "We'd grab blankets and stare up at the sky for hours on summer nights. Fall nights, winter nights. All lot of nights."

So many nights together, innocently enjoying each other's company.

I could tell him right now how much I'd enjoyed being with him.

He watched me. I looked away. *Stop being shy. Just get out with it!*

"It's been nice being back." *Nice.* Hello, vagueness. Nice could mean anything.

He opened the truck door. "It's been nice having you back, too. It's like being kids again, but better since we don't have curfew. Even though I'm headed to bed by nine-thirty." He laughed. "Anyway, it's good to feel part of the family again. I missed it."

Part of the family. Right.

"Like having my kid sister home again."

The words hit like a brick. Numbness stunned my body. *Kid sister.* Ethan...he thought of me as his extended family. As both child *and* a sister.

What did I expect? If we kept acting like old times, then nothing would change. I hadn't realized until now how much I wanted things to change.

I quickly recovered and threw a light punch to his arm. "Yup. Just like old times!" My voice shrill, my thoughts manic. HE THINKS OF ME AS A SISTER. And here I'd been daydreaming about covering myself in more flour for a sexy baking session.

Ethan disappeared into his truck, leaving me with his coat and a certainty that anything between us had all been in my head.

Chapter 12

Ethan

I banged my fist against the steering wheel. I was an idiot.

The dumbest words in history just left my mouth. I actually told Marlowe I thought of her like a kid sister. That hadn't been true since I was what, twelve? And even then, I hadn't viewed her like a sibling. She'd always been special. A friend, but more.

All the time we'd been spending together lately had reminded me of old times. A comfortable existence. Simple even.

The thoughts racing through my head were anything but.

Maybe I'd blurted what I assumed Marlowe wanted to hear. Maybe my subconscious wanted to protect me from a fall. Yeah, I'd taken a psych class in community college. Not like it helped make much sense of myself.

Regardless, dumb move. She played along, but I couldn't imagine she liked being labeled a sister by me. Let alone a kid. If I was lumped in with the Holly family, that made what we had less special. It would send her packing for sure.

At home, I wrote her a text about taking back the sister comment. Deleted it. Wrote it again. My stomach knotted.

I wrote another text and hit send. *I know you're not my sister*

Ugh, no. I should delete—

Marlowe: *Whew. Glad you cleared that up!*

Marlowe: *That'll save me the cost of a pesky DNA test*

Okay, she was taking the high road here. Sparing me. Or hopefully, she hadn't read into what I said and this was all a big overreaction on my part.

Marlowe: *I don't want to be your sister*

My heart bottomed out. I definitely did not want to be related to her. Not by blood.

Me: *I don't want that either. I like what we have. And you're not a kid.*

I paced the room waiting on her response.

Marlowe: *Thanks. I like what we have too. You've always been more special to me than a brother.*

I could breathe again. She'd always been special, and now, I wasn't sure what that meant for us. Maybe it didn't mean anything more than a business arrangement, and we'd continue on as close friends.

Forcing myself to get to sleep, I dreamed of more. Even when I tried not to, my brain filled in the details of a happy life with the only person I'd ever imagined a future with.

"Get your head out of the clouds!"

That would be my dad, interrupting my thoughts. Rightly so, since he was talking to me about this weekend's farm festivities while my mind drifted to everything Marlowe.

"Sorry." I ran a hand across my face, feeling my restless night of sleep taking its toll. "I've got it covered."

Dad grunted. "You've been missing in action a few times this week. Everything okay?"

Instantly, guilt hit. We had seasonal staff this time of year to keep up with the tree sales, but he was right to call me out. Because Dad assumed the best, he didn't instantly conclude I'd cut out of work early to spend time with the girl who got away. "Everything's fine. The Saturday event is good to go. It practically runs on autopilot."

Each year over the second Saturday of December, we ran a small event featuring wagon rides, a craft station for kids run by a local volunteer group, and a single food truck offering hot chocolate and fun-flavored doughnuts.

I took in the farm. Once we had more space, we could amp up our event. A line of food trucks. More kid crafts and more decorations to sell aside from the trees. Actual tree farm merch like T-shirts. My parents liked what we had now—small and manageable. They couldn't envision the bigger picture.

"Been seeing more of your brother lately than you," Dad said. "Thought it odd is all."

Rob agreed to fill in the gaps Saturday while I went to the Tasty Bake competition with Marlowe. It wouldn't be much of an issue anyway. The baking competition happened earlier in the day. I'd only miss an hour or two tops of the afternoon event at the farm. No big deal.

Dad mumbled a few instructions I already knew by heart before taking off. He had a point. I needed to focus. He just didn't need to know where my focus landed.

· ❤ · ❤ · ❤ · ❤ · ❤ ·

The following day was game time. Tasty Bake time.

I headed to Marlowe's house—well, her family's house, it wasn't hers yet. Inside, I helped prepare the cake for transport like we'd researched online. The cake was fortified with toothpicks and set on a non-slip baking mat inside a cardboard bakery box. This cake would *not* slide. Google, thank you for your service.

Marlowe looked me over. "You seem stressed."

"I do? I'm not stressed." Buzzing with excitement, more like. Possibly annoyed at texts about farm stuff I'd already went over with Rob in detail when I wanted my focus on the competition. I texted my brother *Figure it out* to a question he should have known the answer to. "Everything's good. Ready to go?"

Returning to my truck, we headed into downtown Crystal Cove.

I glanced over at my now familiar passenger. "You're not going to complain about the music?"

Marlowe didn't answer right away, letting the 1940s crooner belt out his holiday jingle. "I don't hate this one. It's charming."

Progress. Definite progress.

"You're sure you're okay?" she asked.

I had a lot on my mind. More than usual. "Hey, I'm sorry again about calling you—"

"It's fine," she cut in. "I know you didn't really mean it."

"You do?"

She took on the physical posture of the world *duh*. "Ethan. You know I hate being called a kid and you've never once called me your sister. We got into a familiar groove this week and my guess is that sort of popped out."

I sighed in relief. "That's *exactly* what happened."

Plus the whole brain protecting me thing. Last night I'd startled awake from some random noise, only to toss and turn, dreaming of

Marlowe living her best life somewhere else without me. What was my problem? I rarely dreamed at all or remembered my dreams. It was like my whole life had upturned and even my brainwaves were out of whack.

We arrived to the town square. Visitors already packed the sidewalk surrounding the holiday shops. This would be a busy weekend for tourists getting their dose of holiday action.

A large white tent stood at one end of the square welcoming us with greenery garlands, red bows, and white lights. A decorated Christmas tree greeted us inside the tent, courtesy of Sawyer Farms. We were directed to a line of tables to set up the cakes.

I found our spot and carefully placed the cake box on the table. "Landing confirmed."

Marlowe's cousin Riley approached holding a covered cake carrier. "Congrats on the bake sale win. You two make a good team."

Was that a compliment? I glanced to Marlowe.

"Grans seemed in her prime." Marlowe set aside our bag of emergency supplies. "I doubt she actually cares about the points."

Riley let out her breath in a whoosh. "You know, I was thinking the same. She's always deferring to that teenager for the judging criteria. I swear, they are making it all up as they go."

Marlowe laughed. "Yeah, I wouldn't put it past her." She eyed Riley's container. "What did you make?"

"Peppermint cream cake. I wanted to do a lemon layer cake, but Reece here reminded me lemons are for summer."

Riley's daughter, who'd been lurking behind her mother, perked up. "Rookie mistake, Mom. You don't stand a chance at winning without me."

Marlowe and I laughed. Riley scowled, but there was no bite there. "Watch it, kiddo. How about you? What did you make?"

"A Victoria spiced sponge cake with berry jam filling."

Riley took this in. "I have no idea what that is. I'm used to baking from a box mix."

"See how *desperately* she needs me?" Reece exclaimed.

"I started with a yule log but gave up." Marlowe made a face. "Too lumpy."

It seemed their competitive attitudes had cooled a bit, which was probably a good thing.

More bakers arrived to set up cakes for the tasting and judging. This was an actual competition with judges hired from local restaurants, the downtown bakery, and for whatever reason, the school board.

We had a great classic cake with a good shot at placing well. Marlowe wore another holiday sweater, probably another borrow from her grandmother. Maybe Marlowe was getting closer to liking holiday festivities after all.

My phone buzzed in my back pocket. It'd been buzzing for a few minutes, but I'd ignored it to help Marlowe lift the cake from the box onto the display table.

Buzz buzz.

I glanced at my phone—my brother. I walked out of the tent to take the call. "What's up?"

"Dude, you haven't been answering."

"I told you, I'm at the baking event."

"Doesn't matter. Look, it's Dad. He fell at the farm. It's not good. He's at the hospital."

Chapter 13

Marlowe

Now that the cake arrived at its final destination, I adjusted the finishing touches. Holly leaves, chocolate trees from a candy mold, and crimson winter berries made of fondant—all edible.

Ethan rushed into the tent. "Marlowe, I'm so sorry. I have to go."

I smiled at him. "I think we're all set. You shouldn't have to get an extra tablecloth after all—"

"No, uh, it's my dad. He fell. At the farm."

Reality pounded its way through. "W...what? Is he okay?"

His gaze flitted everywhere but me. "He's in the hospital. I don't have much to go on yet, but they need help at the farm."

"Oh." I nodded. "You're going to the hospital first?"

He tapped his phone's screen. "My mom texted. She said go to the farm. She'll keep me updated if Dad needs surgery." He slipped the phone into his back pocket.

"There's staff at the farm already, right?"

Annoyance flashed across his face. "It's the second Saturday in December."

I racked my brain for any hint of what he was talking about.

Realizing I had no idea of the significance of his statement, he went on. "The farm does a holiday event the second weekend in December. Wagon rides, kid's games, a raffle for a free tree. It starts in an hour."

"Sorry, I didn't know." My clueless questioning would only hold him up. "Just go. I'll check in later."

He blinked in thought before placing a hand at my back. "Hey, no need to say sorry. I didn't tell you about the event at the farm because I assumed it was handled. You'll do great with the cake."

For a moment, he paused, his face so close to mine it caused my breath to cease. And then he was gone.

Ethan's absence hit me like a physical force, as if all the energy propelling me had vanished.

Everything would be fine. Just like Ethan promised. I could handle a baking competition. After all, we'd already done the hard part by delivering the cake in one piece.

I sent up a prayer of healing thoughts for his father. For the tree farm event Ethan hadn't even mentioned until now.

He should have told me. Here I was monopolizing his time when a full-time job required his attention. The literal busiest time of year and I'd snatched him away to manage a cake contest.

I wasn't sure who I was more mad at, him for not telling me or me for not knowing.

Around me, the tables filled with eye-popping creations. A cake in the shape of a Christmas tree, standing vertical with actual twinkle lights wound around it. A bundt cake with a soft dusting of confectioners' sugar and edible greenery along the base. A cake shaped like presents stacked on top of each other. One with a Hanukkah theme where gold glittery frosting dripped down the side of a pristine white layer cake, topped with a menorah-shaped confection.

Shawn arrived with a hearty German chocolate layer cake surrounded by an honest-to-goodness holiday village made of cookies across a giant serving tray. Was that cheating? All those extra cookies that weren't even part of the cake? It definitely looked like cheating.

Rafe and his family presented a tall cake striped in red and white frosting with mini candy canes for edging. An elaborate collection of candy canes adorned the top. Okay now. That cake had to be from a professional bakery.

I met Rafe's gaze across the tent. A smug smile appeared. He knew that cake was amazing. The smug shifted to a sneer when he eyed my cake. How dare he!

Ashe, Cara, and the kids carried in a humble looking yule log. Lumpy like the ones I'd made in my practice runs. At least I had an edge over them.

Given my family's contributions and Riley's on-the-plain-side peppermint cake, I had a decent chance at scoring high points against them. Rafe's cake was the one to beat, unless Shawn's tasted amazing or the judges gave bonus points for all those cookies.

Yeah, I was still in this.

A towering snowflake monstrosity entered the tent carried by two men in white gloves and chef coats. Okay, not monstrosity. The cake was gorgeous. All white with ice blue details. Hardened sugar snowflakes and swirly little thingamabobs poking out the top. I didn't even know what those were called.

A South Asian woman in a red wool coat approached. A fancy wool cap tilted on her head just so. "Hello, Miss…" She peered past me to the name plate beside the cake. "Oh, are you part of the Holly family? One of Emmaline's?"

I forced a confident smile. "Yes."

"Wonderful. Do you have the recipe for your cake?"

Panic set in. Was this a quality check? Confirming we'd actually made the cakes? "Uh, I mean, I don't have it with me."

"That's okay. Here." She handed me a business card. "Email when you have it. We list the recipes on the town website after the competition. It's the number one question everyone asks. Last year we had so many people posting 'recipe please' on each photo on the event page, it took the entire website down."

"Yeesh." I'd get on that later.

"Now, name?"

"Marlowe Holly."

She grinned. "Not your name. The cake."

"Oh, sure. It's a holiday Victoria sponge cake."

"Ah, that's the description. We need a name for *your* version of the cake." She continued to look at me expectantly. "It's number seven in the competition instructions."

Dangit. Why hadn't Ethan mentioned we needed a cake name? No, that wasn't fair. Ethan had an emergency and now I needed to handle this. How hard could it be to name a cake? "How about Victoria's Secret Spice."

She arched a slim brow. "Okay." She used permanent marker to complete the name on a festive card she then handed to me. "Set the card in the stand in front of the cake."

I winced looking at the name on the card. Why did I pick a sexy cake name? My cake wasn't sexy. It was *cake*. And named after a stodgy English queen.

Unfortunately, the permanent part of permanent marker meant I was stuck.

Ethan would have had a cake name at the ready. A non-sexy one. But Ethan wasn't here.

And that was totally fine. He had his own life and job. The responsibility of a tree farm rested on his hot, toned shoulders. Meanwhile, I couldn't properly *name a cake*.

Ethan had already helped me so much. I should have known the tree farm had a big event planned this weekend. I didn't remember the farm hosting a special day when I'd lived here. Obviously, the business had grown in recent years.

I'd only been focused on myself and these silly competitions. All for a house I wasn't sure what I'd even do with. Sure, I technically needed a place to live and didn't have much to go back to in California, but I hadn't decided yet what I'd do if I won.

Even more, what would I do if I didn't win?

What was I *doing*?

My thoughts fogged into a thick soup. Quite the opposite of a delightful, fluffy cake.

All through the introductions from the judges and the initial rounds of photographs, I operated on autopilot. The foggy thoughts tinged darker. I should have been helping Ethan at the farm. Surely a better use of my time. My cake had no real chance of winning.

I was spiraling. And not a cake decorating kind of spiral.

The competition passed in a blur. The cakes were sliced into and sampled by each judge. Grans and her own slate of scorekeepers had arrived, watching every detail unfold.

I kept glancing to my right, then my left, each time chastising myself for the automatic disappointment that hit when Ethan wasn't here. Had I been relying on him too much already?

Yes. The answer was yes.

The snowflake monstrosity took first place. No surprise.

"The sugar work alone!" The head judge, a Julia Child clone with wild dark curls who led the town council, oozed enthusiasm. "And it tasted *spectacular*."

Second place, startlingly, went to Riley and her daughter Reece's peppermint cake.

"Simple, but perfectly executed," the Julia Child-esque judge announced.

The loudest cheers came from Reece. "Yes! Peppermint Domination!"

She'd named the cake too.

Riley gasped and jumped up and down screaming. She flung her arms around her daughter and they jumped in celebration together. The crowd snapped photos, murmuring over the sweetness of the mother-daughter duo.

They were so cute I couldn't help but smile at their victory. Across the tent, Grans beamed with pride.

No one else in the family placed in the main competitive category. Ashe and crew received a consolatory honor for Best Tasting Traditional Holiday Cake. Shawn received second place honorary mention for Most Elaborate Cakescape, which someone had to have made up five minutes ago.

A judge handed me a generic ribbon with the words: *Crystal Cove Tasty Bake Competition Participant.*

Beautiful. A participation ribbon.

Ashe and Shawn gathered at my table looking defeated. I felt their defeat. "Looks like we got outbaked."

Shawn glowered. "I can't believe I took vacation days to make this. Anybody want some cookies? There are eighty of them. I counted."

Ashe looked past me. "Where's your shadow?"

I shot him a warning glare but answered anyway. "He's at the farm."

"Makes sense. Second Saturday of December."

Did everyone know the significance of this date but me?

"We're headed there now with the kids," Ashe said. "Want to ride with us?"

I wanted to. I'd come here with Ethan, so I didn't have my car. But that murky cloud of thoughts weighed heftier than ever. Ethan had real work to do, and now an emergency with his father. The last thing he needed was me hanging around and getting in the way.

"I'll ride home with Grans," I told them.

Chapter 14

Ethan

Dad had a fractured ankle. Not as bad as a broken leg, but the recovery time meant he'd be off his feet for weeks. The remaining holiday season.

Mom went into nurse mode, making sure Dad followed the doctor's orders. We weren't above hiding the keys to his truck so he wouldn't leave the house. So far, he'd conceded. He could at least do administrative work from home on his laptop.

Which left me and Rob to keep business going at the farm. To prep for winter, and of course, sell Christmas trees.

I hadn't seen Marlowe since the baking competition. When I'd ditched her. I'd texted her an apology and an update on Dad. She told me she understood—family came first. She hadn't placed in the competition and now we were behind in points. I should have been there. I'd signed on to help her and couldn't follow through.

Today, traffic at the farm was slow with only a few folks trickling in this afternoon.

"Do you have a gift shop?" A fashionable blond woman probably in her thirties looked past me toward the barn.

"Sorry, no. We have wreaths and greens over here." I showed her to the small collection of pre-made porch pots and door wreaths. We hired a part-timer to assemble them. Though, we'd underestimated demand and were low on stock already.

She looked over the scant offerings. "Hmm. Okay. I thought you had more shopping at the main farm." She tapped at her phone. "This website has your farm marked as selling 'holiday fare' other than trees. I'll send in a correction."

She circled back toward the parking lot.

Dangit. She looked like she might spend some real money on holiday fare. If we only had any.

Rob walked over and freed an earbud from his ear, letting the thin cord dangle over his sweatshirt. "Let me guess. She's looking for a gift shop. Don't they get the sign says *tree farm?* We're not Mall of Middle America here."

I moved a few of the decorative pots closer together so the display didn't look so ransacked. "Other farms offer more besides the trees. It's not out of the question."

"Where would we put a gift shop?"

"We could use the barn. Go for a rustic look. Move everything in the barn to a new, modernized outbuilding."

Rob eyed me with suspicion. "Sounds like you've thought this through. With Dad's body breaking down, don't you think we should consider selling?"

"Nope." I angled past him toward the office.

Rob jogged to catch up. "Why not? Mom's been looking for a reason to sell, and this might be it with Dad out of commission at home. Do you want to do this for the rest of your life?"

I stopped. My brother and I were different people, but we'd always shown up when it came to the farm and our family. Now that we were older, we needed to secure the family business long term. Which required new ideas, not giving up. Sure, Rob dreamed of, well, I wasn't sure what he dreamed about. But he sure was working less on farm business and more on his own creative projects.

"I know you don't, but I do," I told him.

"Do you really?"

"What's with you? Of course I do."

"Look, even Dad's saying it's probably time."

Now that wasn't true. No way. "There's no chance Dad said he wants to sell. He's in a lot of pain right now and feeling helpless." I swung open the screen door to the office trailer and the craziest thing happened. The whole door came off the hinges. I held an entire door in my hand.

Rob cracked up laughing. "It's like the universe giving us a sign. We're literally falling apart."

I leaned the dislodged door upright against the building's worn siding. "When we expand, we'll have plenty of room for a gift shop and more trees for more sales. And we don't need to replace this screen door. The exterior door works fine enough."

I welcomed the warmth of the office after working outside for hours. Rob opened the office fridge and took out a couple of sodas.

He handed one to me. "You think you're going to get the Hollys to fork over their land? I know you and Marlowe have a thing, but don't get your hopes up."

Rob was the only person I'd told about the arrangement since he knew most of it from the night at Checkers. And he'd grilled me about what I'd been doing with Marlowe lately.

"If we win, that's our deal. She sells us the land." I sounded defensive and I knew it.

"*If* you win. And if you get a bank loan. And if she follows through on her promise."

"Why don't you think she'll follow through?" I was definitely defensive now.

He took a swig of his drink. "Are you kidding me? Marlowe Holly? Her entire history with you is turning you down or running off."

"That's not true. Not even a little." I'd never found the courage to ask her out for her to turn me down. Nope—just pined after her like a lovesick schoolboy. Now, a lovesick grown boy.

The desk phone rang. I ignored it. "Marlowe didn't run off. She went to college."

"And never came back. You gonna get that?" Rob nodded toward the phone.

"You get it."

"Fine." He grabbed the phone. "Yeah. Uh huh. I know. Told him as much. I will. Okay. See ya." He hung up. "That was Dad. He said close up at six today, not seven."

"Absolutely not. We'll lose money."

"Have you looked at the data? We don't sell much past six. The lot by the highway does but not the farm."

The data. Who was this brother of mine suddenly caring about data? "Are you and Dad having conversations about the farm without me? I told you I've got a plan."

"You don't listen. I do."

I held myself back from lunging at him. Big brother energy gone wild. "Did Dad actually say he wants to sell?" That would be a total one-eighty from anything he'd said before.

"Honestly, my guess is he's hanging onto the business for you."

"Or, you know, because it's the business he and Mom built, and it's their paycheck. Maybe that reason."

Rob had the nerve to roll his eyes. "Dad could have sold years ago and taken a job with the Tanaka's garden center."

"Working for someone else?" I snorted. "Hardly."

He shook his head. "Dad's been hanging on so he won't disappoint you."

"He's against every idea I come up with to improve business. Why would he hang on, but insist on not changing anything?" The man was more stubborn than a mule with its feet sunk in concrete. "None of this selling the business makes sense."

"I never said he made sense." Rob shrugged. "He's been looking at his options. Sell the farm and retire. Live the good life. Go on a cruise."

My head spun. Dad never cared about vacations or cruises. His idea of a good time was the county fair. More daring, a county fair across the border in Wisconsin.

Rob picked a fresh pair of work gloves from a bin on a low cabinet. "You can do anything you want. Anything. Anywhere. Do you want that anything to be a tree farm in the only town you've ever lived in?"

He patted me on the back, and I could practically feel his pity shedding on me. He left the office, closing the door gently behind him.

I liked Crystal Cove. I liked running into familiar faces around town. I knew what to expect from just about everything since not a whole lot changed. That made it easier to face what did need to change. Like our farm. I wanted the business to keep going, to keep our family history going forward.

I sat at the table off the office kitchen and let my mind wander. The first trail my thoughts picked up involved the one person never too far from my mind. And how I needed her more than ever.

Chapter 15

Marlowe

I checked with Ethan first before coming out to the farm. With his dad injured, Ethan likely altered his work schedule. While I didn't want to be in the way, I also didn't want to ignore him. He needed to know I could do more of the holiday activity planning on my own.

Ethan's face lit with a smile when I found him in the farm office. He abandoned his cardboard cup of coffee and threw an arm around me.

"Just the person I wanted to see. Come here." He ushered me to the table in the kitchenette where a magazine lay open.

My body buzzed from the lingering pressure of his partial embrace. Even a half hug and I turned to mush.

"Here's what we should do for the gingerbread contest. I've already put in an order for priority shipping for the isomalt."

The magazine page displayed a Victorian house made of gingerbread and sugary confections. Little gumdrop bushes dotted the perimeter and the windows appeared to be lit from within.

"Hollybrooke House," he announced, since I hadn't responded. "That's what we make for the contest."

"You want *us* to make *that*?" I pointed. "I'm a far cry from a professional baker, Ethan. I'm not even like those home bakers competing for a cake plate in a hot tent. Besides, I don't even know what ice melt is."

"*Isomalt.* It's a sugar substitute. It melts and looks like glass. Remember, everything has to be edible."

I did not remember everything had to be edible because I couldn't seem to retain the extensive list of rules. We'd never win this competition when the very thought of it made me want to dive into a warm, dark closet. "How much time do we have?"

"The gingerbread contest is in two weeks, right before Christmas. Next up this coming weekend is the Holly Days' Family Fest. Relay races, obstacle course, snowman building contest. You know, the family team stuff."

Right.

"You don't remember." He unfolded Grans' list of activities. "Then mandatory caroling."

"*Mandatory caroling?* I have to draw the line at forced communal signing." Too far. This was all too far.

Then again, the house. The reason for doing any of this.

He laughed. "You're an alto, right? You're good at blending. I remember middle school choir."

I covered my face with my hands. "Don't remind me."

We'd been required to "audition" in front of the class for a grade, even though every student ended up singing in *Rockford of Ages* at the mall in Rockford, the pinnacle showbiz event for middle school choirs in the farthest reaches of northern Illinois. The audition had been intended to prepare us for the big-time.

All I'd known then was I hated singing alone and especially alone on command.

I'd frozen. Worse: I'd even practiced in front of my dresser mirror and wasn't as bad as I'd feared.

But up there on the fake stage in the classroom facing everyone I'd grown up with, I freaked. I'd freaked so hard I fled the room in tears, without even uttering a single note. Which made the embarrassment so much worse.

"Marlowe." Ethan's gentle hand returned me to the present. "You're not twelve anymore. The caroling is pretty casual. You can mouth *watermelon* over and over if you want to look like you're singing."

I sank into a chair. "I'm being dramatic. Sorry." I flipped through the magazine. The gingerbread creations were artistic masterpieces.

Ethan shoved the magazine aside. "Here, look." His phone appeared in front of me. "These are pictures of last year's contest on the town website. To get an idea what we're up against."

While not the perfection displayed in the magazine, the submissions were incredibly creative.

My shoulders sank. Then again, I only had to beat my family, not everybody in town. Then again: part two: the kids factoring in upped the ante. Riley's daughter, Reece, had baking skills she could bring to the gingerbread contest. "This looks like it will take months. Is there a kit or something?"

"No kit will do this, but I did find blueprints online."

"Blueprints?" Blueprints. For a cookie house. "Don't you have work to do?" Guilt crept in for taking Ethan's time. "I promise I'll do the bulk of the gingerbread thingy so you have more time at the farm."

He blinked, seeming to focus on me rather than the edible blueprints in his mind. No, the blueprints weren't edible. Just the building. "We're in this together, Marlowe. You know that." He looked at me closer. "Is everything okay?"

"Yes." No. Nothing was okay. "I just…" I found myself clamming up like usual. My fallback to pretend everything was fine and chipper, full steam ahead!

"I have an idea." He held a hand out to me. "Let's take a walk through the farm. We can catch the frost on the branches before the sky clears up and the sun melts it away."

Okay, that sounded almost…romantic.

I put on my gloves and followed Ethan outside. We approached the barn, weathered but sturdy, a fixture of my childhood. Not much appeared to be different around here. He'd said his parents were resistant to change. If their resistance risked the business itself, that made for a real challenge. Losing the tree farm would be a major blow for Ethan.

He led me into the barn. "I made myself a woodworking station over here. Small, but it gets the job done."

A wooden sign hung above the work bench carved with the words Sawyer Woodworking Inc. I nodded toward the sign. "Your second career?"

"Nah. Just something I do for fun. I made those shelves over there. Half my apartment is furniture I've scrapped together. If I nick the wood so it's not good enough to sell, I'm the only one who'll notice."

"You sell your work?" He'd always been crafty with wood, doing projects for 4-H as a kid.

He shrugged. "A few things here and there at a local shop."

We left the barn and progressed through a gate into the tree farm itself. Rows of frost-tipped evergreens greeted us. "How's your dad doing?" I asked.

"He's alright. Working on the books from home. Ordering us around using every form of technology available." He grinned. "As long as he doesn't show up here and risk injury, he can send me as many texts as he wants."

Our boots crunched against the lightly frozen ground. The crisp air tickled my nose and woke me from my cloudy thoughts. But to truly feel free of the clouds, I needed to further process.

"I feel a little let down about some things," I admitted. "I didn't tell you this because it's embarrassing. I offered to volunteer again at the respite center, but they need a six-month commitment. I can't commit when I don't know what's beyond these next few weeks."

He slowed his pace. "Marlowe. You're enough as you are. Right now."

"I wasn't asking whether I was enough for anybody."

"The way you described it, you're a failure because you can't commit to the volunteer role. You're facing a lot of changes. It's okay to not have it all figured out."

"I know," I snapped. My own sharp tone surprised me. "Sorry. I didn't mean to sound so defensive."

Ethan stopped. "You're hard on yourself. You always have been. I just can't figure out why. Your family loves you regardless of what you accomplish. You know that, right?"

"Yes."

Of course they did. They'd told me as much.

"Then what is it?" he pressed.

Deep down, I knew my family would forever view me as the baby who needed coddling and special treatment. Hadn't I proved over and over how much I didn't need them? That I could stand on my own?

Why couldn't they believe it?

No. Why couldn't *I* believe it?

I glared at Ethan. "I hate when you're right, you know."

He reached his hand to mine. "It's a tough life, being right so often."

His joking didn't lessen the skip in my heart. The pulse of heat through his touch injected helium into my thoughts, making my head feel light as air. I smiled, a genuine smile.

But the happy moment was fleeting. Those murky, ocean-deep thoughts lurked. "Okay, truth? I'm finding it hard to know what to do with my life and what to make of myself."

Big understatement. I hadn't admitted this out loud to anyone. "California has been my home since I started grad school, and here I am graduated and a few years into a career, but it still feels...temporary. I can't explain it any other way. I've always had a goal. Get into my top choice colleges. Graduate with honors. Ace the entry exams for grad school. Get accepted into a good graduate program. Achieve my degree and find a great job. Excel at my job and get promoted." My breath puffed into a cloud in the cold air. "Then it all stopped."

I looked at him, waiting for an impatient glance at his phone. Ethan watched me with what I could only surmise was active interest.

"I never imagined it stopping. That feeling of anticipation about the next thing to do. The next thing to achieve. I wasn't supposed to *lose* the job." I sighed. "You'd think my next big thing would be to get a bigger, better job." This was the hardest part to admit. "I don't know if I want that anymore."

"Your worth isn't dependent on your job." A soft beam of sun hit his face from an opening in the clouds. "Or anything you accomplish. You're special because you're you. You always have been."

I wanted to laugh him off. The Holly name was supposed to mean I was special, but it had often weighed me down like a burden.

"Hey, I mean it. You're not your family. You're you."

Ethan looked at me fully, deeply, wholly. He saw me. He always had. As kids, he'd been my ally, and a bit of hired muscle when I needed it against my brothers. But in high school, something shifted. I doubted myself and questioned my identity. Cue the dark clothes and hanging with outcasts and shy wallflowers. Because despite feeling loved and included in my larger-than-life family, I began to believe there really was something wrong with me. That I was tainted. Scarred. An oddball who would forever be marked by my tragic beginnings. How could I ever outgrow the label other people placed on me?

To correct that, my only option was to leave them all behind.

I'd believed my own dark thoughts, the doubt, instead of the people who loved me. Instead of Ethan, who'd been a support even when I'd walked away.

He was here now. Taking time away from the job that needed him, during the busiest time of the year. And still, I clung to those dark thoughts and beliefs. Why?

"Why have you believed in me for so long?" I asked him. "Why, when I haven't been the friend you needed?"

He paused before answering. "Because love isn't conditional."

A perfectly reasonable sentiment. One I had trouble digesting no matter how hard I tried.

Ethan appeared to freeze in place, as if startled by something. I turned. "What? What's behind me?"

"No, it's nothing." He abruptly turned toward the gate. "We should probably get back. It's cold out here."

Chapter 16

Ethan

I'd declared my love for Marlowe Holly. *To* Marlowe Holly.

Just said it. Right out loud.

She either hadn't heard me or kept tight-lipped to spare my feelings. We walked to her car in silence. I had a good lead on her so she couldn't see my face.

Love isn't conditional. I couldn't love Marlowe any less if I tried. The memories, there were so many of them, and they'd all rushed back the second she showed up at that bar.

"I'll pick up the rest of the gingerbread materials," Marlowe was saying as she opened the car door.

I couldn't read her thoughts at all. Marlowe had a way of making up for showing any vulnerability by immediately locking down tight. The opposite of me, turned out.

"Are you okay, Ethan?"

Did you not hear me declare my love for you?

She looked at me, open. Blank. Guarded? Or clueless?

Maybe she hadn't heard the word *love* at all. Maybe she'd assumed I'd repeated a familiar phrase. Did it only count if I'd said *I love you*, in that order?

"I'll text you about the next event," I stammered. The competition. Safe territory. "See ya."

I swore a hint of disappointment came through when I sent her off. Then again, Marlowe couldn't stand the holidays and I'd just saddled her with shopping for more baking. Funny, given holidays and baking were exactly what brought us together again.

In the following days, Marlowe didn't bring up my love declaration so I didn't either. I was probably overreacting. Love being unconditional was a thing people said. Even to friends. A normal, not-meaning-any-thing-more-than-that kind of statement.

Meanwhile, renewed determination struck. I would change Marlowe's outlook on the holidays. I planned to use my time intentionally to do it.

Having plenty of downtime each weekday, Marlowe offered to hang out with me at the tree farm during working hours. The day began cold, colder than it had been all month. Marlowe's nose turned pink and she stomped her feet to keep warm.

"You can go inside the office and warm up." I felt bad having her stand outside helping customers with trees, but she'd insisted.

"I'm good." She smiled at me.

My brother helped a familiar family carry their chosen tree to their van. "Ethan, how are you? Good to see you." The woman, a white blond in her late thirties, stopped at the counter by the gate where we took payments.

"Hey, same, Sherry. I'm good. Looks like you got a great tree."

She recounted how the kids ran through every row of available trees until landing on their chosen one. "We've been so busy with the office expansion we haven't decorated at home," she said. "Did your dad let you know about the position?"

I nodded. I kept my voice low and my response to the point as I thanked her for her interest, and the tree, and moved on to the next customer.

We hit a lull and Marlowe wandered over. "What position was your friend talking about?"

I'd hoped she hadn't noticed. "It's nothing. Sherry and her husband run a local business. Home renovation. They recently expanded into exteriors."

"You help build houses in your free time, so that makes sense."

"Yeah, but I'm not interested."

She didn't say anything.

"Because I have a job. Here. At the farm."

"Why would your dad have talked to them about a job if you already have one working for him?"

She could put two and two together. Still, I answered. "Dad thinks he's being clever turning my interest away from the farm so he can spring selling it on me and not feel bad."

"He wants to sell?"

I hated how Rob was right. Dad had been exploring part-time work for retirement. And I caught him bookmarking cruises on a travel deals website. "His latest injury apparently put thoughts in his head about retiring."

She didn't press, but her unasked questions rang in my mind anyway.

After we closed for the night, I took Marlowe on a holiday lights tour through the local neighborhoods, with our trusty soundtrack the holiday radio station. Since Crystal Cove was V.I.C., aka Very Into Christmas, lots of houses went all out. Which could mean a front lawn filled with inflatable holiday yard decorations or thousands of lights covering the house and shrubbery. Every so often, we'd spot something simple like a red ribbon-trimmed wreath on the door with a spotlight pointed at it.

Marlowe chattered beside me in the passenger seat, scoring the decorations based on her own highly specific criteria. She didn't complain once about the music.

"Okay, you're either going to love this next one or hate it." I headed out of the neighborhood to a stretch of country road.

She squinted through the dark. "Uh, what is that?"

The glow ahead was impossible to miss. A beacon in the night.

"Why is the car ahead of us slowing?" Her tone filled with dread.

I tapped the truck's stereo to forward to another station. I slowed behind the line of cars and watched for Marlowe's reaction.

On time with the music, the house in the distance pulsed with light. Red, green, red and green together, then every color imaginable shining with precise, digital delight. We inched forward, gaining a closer view.

"The house and the music. It's all synced together?"

I beamed at her. "Isn't it the coolest?"

We'd come in halfway through the spectacle, so the big finale with Santa and his reindeer along the top of the house went disco-wild, flashing and blinking along with the frantic music.

Cars honked and kids whooped cheers out of rolled-down windows.

The house darkened, but only for a handful of seconds. The show was about to start again.

We moved forward as the cars ahead of us cleared out. Now we were positioned right in front of the house.

Marlowe's mouth hung open. Slowly, she folded herself inward. At one point, she covered her eyes. "It's so...bright. And intrusive."

"Did you see the little Christmas village in the side yard? It looks like it's supposed to be a miniature Crystal Cove."

Marlowe's face morphed into a slow but unmistakable scowl.

She hated this. Like, absolutely loathed it.

The music escalated as it neared the big ending. "This is the part we saw already," she said. "When we first drove up."

Meaning, *I'm done now.*

I sighed. With no one idling ahead of us, we were free to leave. "You know, people come from two counties over to see this house."

"Really? Two whole counties?"

"Maybe one county," I grumbled. I moved us toward the end of the road until we reached a stop sign. A sign I should take to heart beyond my driving. "Look, I'm sorry. I wanted you to see the holidays through my eyes."

"You liked that back there?"

I shut off the radio. "Yeah."

Even if we won the competition, and Marlowe owned Hollybrooke House, we weren't exactly a matched set when it came to our interests. A good chunk of my life revolved around holidays. I made my living at it. Marlowe couldn't stand the things that made me happy.

"I'll take you home." I hit the blinker to turn left toward the house.

"Hey." She laid a hand on my arm. "I like driving with you. I'm not into Christmas lights bright enough to be seen from another solar system, but I don't need to go home yet."

"Are you sure? I don't want to make you miserable."

"Like that's possible. Keep on driving, Sawyer."

It's impossible for me to make her miserable. That's what she was saying. "Well, okay then. Turning right, it is."

I headed toward downtown. "Do you put up a tree at home?" I asked her.

She responded with a look I couldn't suss out. "Anna has a small one. It sits on a table with the lights and ornaments already on it."

"That counts."

"I never meant to hate the holidays, you know. It just feels excessive to me. Too much for one day that goes by in a blink."

I slowed as the speed limit lowered. The downtown shopping district lit up like a, well, Christmas tree. Thousands of lights adorned storefronts. Decorative snowflakes illuminated lampposts and every store window featured a themed display. "Festive, but less of a spectacle. Not as bad as the house?"

"It's nice. If you like this sort of thing." Her voice had a detached tone. "I know you're trying to make me like the holidays again."

"Yeah." I could admit it. "I like sharing this with you."

She went quiet again.

"I drive past Hollybrooke House even when it's out of the way."

She snapped her head toward me. "You do?"

"Yeah. Good memories. Plus the house is pretty, you know? It makes me think of..." I cleared my throat. "You. It reminds me of you."

I stared at the road. I didn't dare look at her. I wasn't prepared.

Once Christmas ended and the new year crept in, would I pass the house with the same good memories? Maybe I'd be heartbroken and need a detour.

I didn't want to ask. I wanted to live in the moments we had and not question what lay ahead.

If Marlowe lost the house, I had no idea if she'd stay. If she won, she still might not stay. Maybe this was all too much and she'd be more than eager to get back home.

Her home wasn't here. Her home was in California, no matter how much she doubted herself. That was reality. She might plan to pack up her West Coast life and return here, only to find some new opportunity and flip to a new direction. She'd leave me behind all over again.

The farm expansion would require a new plan, depending on which Holly family the house went to. I had no guarantee my life would be anywhere close to the same this time next year.

With no more town to show off, I drove us to her house. I rolled to a stop in the driveway.

She didn't leave the truck. "Want to come inside?"

Yes. "I don't know. It's late."

"It's only a quarter past eight. Aren't you hungry? Grans has way too much food. It's a problem if no one eats it." She grinned at me. Mischievous like the Marlowe I once knew. "Besides, we're supposed to be dating. Shawn is staying at the house now after checking out of his hotel. It will be good cover if he sees us together."

Good cover. That's all the invitation was.

"Hey." Her voice came softer. "Honestly, I don't care about Shawn seeing us. I want to hang out. Watch movies. Eat junk food. Like the old days. Please?"

As if I could say no. I could never say no to Marlowe.

Chapter 17

Marlowe

Having Ethan over just for fun—not making plans using confection-themed blueprints or swarmed by Hollys during a family event—felt like a slice of the happiness we'd taken for granted as kids.

We parked ourselves in the front parlor. The furniture ran more stiff and fancy than the larger family room, but since Shawn had taken that over to watch some reality show about real estate developers, the parlor it would be.

Ethan and I could not decide on a movie. One conversation about a favorite turned into rapid-fire question rounds of which movies we'd seen or not seen the past decade. Which movies were must-watches, which were skips. Our must-sees did not always overlap.

Then we got to TV shows. The best dramas, the best comedies, and which streaming platforms they aired on.

"We're going to need a list." I grabbed a notepad from an antique desk. Holly leaves decorated the corners of the pages. I wrote down our top choices so far.

"Let me see." Ethan peered over my shoulder. "I still can't believe you haven't seen *The Martian*. It's seriously so good. Put it as number one."

"Maybe because I was busy watching every Marvel movie ever made." I spun the pen—also decorated with holly leaves—between my fingers. "Why are there *so* many of them? And why can't I stop watching?"

Finally, after complex elimination rounds, we decided on a movie neither of us had seen, *Crazy Rich Asians.* It was either the best choice or the worst choice for us. Romantic and involving big families while centered around a wedding, it wasn't exactly a holiday romance, but somehow the premise kept reminding me of my own life. Returning home to a family who didn't understand how I'd changed, and me maybe not fully grasping what that meant.

Home. This was my home. No matter how far I'd tried to distance myself, including literal, actual distance, my family and this house were a part of me.

We hunkered down on the couch. It was on the small-ish side to fit the room. The big couch, Shawn had hogged to himself along with the bigger TV. I had my feet tucked underneath me on my side to give Ethan plenty of room on his end, along with a tapestried footstool to stretch his feet.

A half hour into the movie, my legs ached for a stretch. I adjusted my position. Adjusted again.

Ethan shifted too. "You can rest your feet on my lap."

Which would involve touching. Except we were supposed to be dating. Laying my legs on his lap was a totally normal thing to do in our situation. Besides, we used to do this all the time. Back before it meant anything other than simply sharing space on a small couch.

I stretched my legs across his. Totally fine.

Also completely fine when his hand rested on top of my socked foot. I hardly noticed at all. Just his sturdy, tree hauling hand needing some R-and-R.

Another chunk of time passed, when a sensation grazed against my foot. "Eee!" I jerked my foot back.

"Sorry!" Ethan threw his hands up. "I didn't mean to...rub your foot with my hand."

"Is there a such thing as accidental massaging?" He'd stroked my foot. Through a sock, but still.

And I liked it. I didn't want him to stop, but the act surprised me so much, I'd flinched.

"It's actually okay," I said. "It's your loss for touching my dirty sock."

He shook his head, faintly grinning.

We shifted positions a few more times through the movie until I ended up leaning against him. More like I was overtaking the small couch and crushing him into the corner.

A particularly quiet scene on screen caused me sudden and acute awareness of our couch position. He hadn't complained, but this was probably too much. I turned to adjust and my nose met his chin.

"Sorry, I—"

"It's okay," he interrupted.

But there was nowhere for him to go until I moved. And I was sort of stuck in the crack between the cushions. I inched up to free myself from the quicksand couch until our noses aligned at the same level. Which meant our lips aligned as well.

Our lips. A mere breath from each other.

"Hey." He spoke in the quietest voice I'd ever heard from him.

It wasn't a complaining *Hey*. More like a, *Hey, this is new*. Or a, *Hey, hello, you're a single inch from my face.*

I dared not breathe. "Hey."

Ask to kiss me. Tell me you want to kiss me. Just kiss me.

We hovered for another million seconds until I couldn't stand it anymore. I closed the minuscule gap between us.

It was happening. I was kissing Ethan Sawyer.

Ethan kissed me back. Tentative at first but definitely willing. Sure and certain pressure that felt new and familiar at the same time.

His lips were warm and reminded me of home. Like a thousand memories strung together. He tasted faintly of mint. And perfection.

I eased apart from him, out of breath. He looked me in the eyes. Deeply. A nervous energy edged a laugh out of both of us.

So that just happened.

We finished the movie without speaking. Hopefully we'd get a sequel. To the movie. To the kissing too, but I was too freaked to think about it further.

I shut the movie off, stretched, and made a production of yawning. Ethan took the hint. I followed him out to the mudroom area by the side door. He laced up his boots.

"I'm okay with what happened." He stood, coat in hand, because true as he said, the man ran hot. I'd felt those hot lips with my own. Delicious, heated lips that sent shockwaves through me.

"Okay." I didn't know what to say. I wasn't good at this. I wasn't good at this *with Ethan* because we'd never done this before.

One simple kiss and I was struck speechless.

"Maybe we can talk about it more tomorrow?" He nodded in a way to suggest I could nod along with him and understanding would occur.

"Yes. Yes, tomorrow. *Tomorrow.*" Why had I emphasized the word tomorrow like that? I sounded textbook awkward. Look up the word and check out my photo beside the definition. "It's not like I haven't kissed anyone before. I've had boyfriends, you know."

He blinked. "I assume you have. You went out with Blane Chandler, didn't you?"

Blane Chandler, a flash from the past. "His name always sounded to me like a country club or a golf course. *The Blane Chandler Memorial Golf Greens.*" I snickered.

"Marlowe." He stepped closer. "It's okay. What happened doesn't have to mean anything more."

He was absolutely acting more mature about this than me. We were adults. One kiss should not throw me off like this.

But this wasn't merely any kiss from a Blane or a guy from grad school. This was Ethan. *My* Ethan.

This kiss changed everything.

He leaned in and landed a soft peck to my cheek. Sweet and chaste, but it rocked my insides like a hurricane.

"Okay," I said again. "Tomorrow."

Tomorrow came, and Ethan texted first.

Ethan: *Good morning, sweet lips*

No. Absolutely not. I could not handle this so early in the morning.

Ethan: *That was a joke. Ready to talk?*

He wanted to talk about the kiss already? It was—well, it was after nine a.m. I'd slept in. No job, no volunteering, and no holiday shenanigans to start the day.

Okay, I needed to woman up here. I hadn't been ready for this as a teenager. I'd needed to move and experience life apart from what I knew. But now? Now I was ready. Maybe.

As kids, ours was an innocent, friend-centered love. But my love for him grew warmer, deeper, as I'd aged. Only pushing my family away meant by default pushing Ethan away too.

Just because I'd pushed him away didn't mean those embers hadn't been smoldering all that time. I was a messy, untended fire with a momentary spritz of gasoline tossed on it. Thanks a lot, *Crazy Rich Asians.*

Ethan: *I'm ready to talk when you're ready*

Me: *Okay*

I needed to say more than *okay.*

Me: *I'll make plans for us after work. Dinner. Probably not a movie (lol)*

Ethan: *I hope it's a movie*

I grabbed a nearby receipt from my bedside table and fanned myself. It did nothing to cool me off. He hoped it was a movie...did this mean Ethan might feel the same way as me? This was like high school all over again. Except worse because as an adult with a graduate degree who paid taxes, I should not have been reduced to a melting puddle over the potential of *maybe kissing while watching a movie with my crush.*

Ethan: *After all, we need to get through the new* Jurassic Park *movies*

Oh. Right. The movie list. Ethan teasing me yet again.

Perhaps best to lay low from the tree farm today to give us space. Okay, to give *me* space. We had Holly Days festivities this weekend (ugh) plus the gingerbread house to plan, so plenty of prep work needed to be done. Whatever that prep involved. I also needed to do laundry. Lastly, one more task: figure out my life.

See? What a busy schedule. No time to hang out at the tree farm deciphering Ethan's thoughts as he stretched the limits of plaid cotton with his working man's biceps.

Who knew tree hauling was sexy?

"Probably a lot of people, Marlowe," I told myself out loud. "Probably that's why sexy lumberjack calendars exist."

I texted Ethan I'd come by at closing. Which left all day for my supremely busy schedule.

I managed the laundry and an inventory of baking ingredients. A lot of scrolling on the internet. Curious about the history of our family's land, I delved deeper into when and how the area had been settled and which Indigenous tribes had originally lived on the land.

If I ended up with the house, I needed to do something worthwhile with it. I knew in my bones it wasn't enough to simply get the house and land and just hang onto it. What if I could build a park? Or protect the land somehow?

A phone call interrupted my pondering. An unexpected one.

That evening, I arrived at the farm, nervous but antsy to see Ethan. I wasn't sure what to expect. Did we kiss now as a greeting? Cheek or lips? Maybe a simple hug until we talked about the parameters of our kissing. Did we even need to set parameters?

Thankfully, a recent development offered the perfect distraction.

"I have plans for us," I announced once Ethan came within earshot.

He had on his navy blue work coat, this time with a red hooded sweatshirt beneath it. Those precious biceps were all covered up. "Yeah? Are we going to see Santa?"

My smile froze. "What? How did you—did someone tell you?"

Confusion took over. "Tell me what? I was joking about Santa."

Excitement pulsed through me. "Oh, you're going to love this. We're going to *be* Santa."

Confusion continued. "I'm sorry, what? Aren't we grabbing dinner?"

That had been the plan until a happy distraction surfaced in the form of Sheree Bolden from the children's respite center. She'd called in the favor I'd so naively offered. I'd left it pretty open about what I'd been willing to help with.

I hadn't been joking about the Santa. I wish I had. But this task was perfect for Ethan. Besides, no way would I do this by myself. "The respite center's annual holiday event needs a last-minute volunteer after a call-in. So, I said yes."

"To *being* Santa?" Ethan set aside his work gloves at the pay station counter. "Marlowe, playing Santa is serious business. You can't just *be* Santa."

"I'm not going to be anything. I told them you'd do it."

He shook his head. "Walt Jurek plays Santa. For everything in town and two towns over. He owns a professional grade St. Nicolas suit and hires a personal stylist for maintaining his white beard."

"Look, the respite place called for help and mentioned costumes. Maybe I assumed it was Santa?" Clearly out of my depth here.

He cracked a smile. "You have serious avoidance issues. I get it. If the respite center needs help, I'm in. We better head out."

We made it to the center in good time despite a traffic delay leaving town. More oglers to the flashy Christmas lights house, I'd guess. Ethan, to his credit, did not bring up our kiss or the fact I'd trapped him into entertaining children for the night. I would owe him big-time for this.

As it turned out, they had Santa covered. Like Ethan said, playing Santa was no simple task to be parceled out to an unofficial volunteer's fake boyfriend.

No, we would get to play elves. That's right—*we*.

"We're supposed to wear these?" I held up a green hat with snow white trim and a little ball on the end. It matched a green and white full body jumpsuit. All in a plush, emerald velveteen.

"The elf suits were donated." Sheree gestured toward a box labeled Holiday Costumes. "That's what you get for living in a town obsessed with Christmas. Wearing the suit is optional. The hat we prefer you wear. The main job will be assisting Santa and the staff with the donated gifts."

"Oh, I'm wearing the suit." Ethan looked as happy as the kids who'd be gifted presents in a half hour. "And so are you," he told me.

I didn't fight it. After all, the suits were right here. I could manage an evening dressed like an elf to entertain some kids.

And I'd dragged Ethan here. I couldn't let him face elf awareness on his own.

Minutes later, I emerged from the women's bathroom fully dressed in my costume. Technically it fit. A little saggy on the backside and a little slouchy at the ankles. Green wasn't exactly my best color, what choice did I have.

Ethan appeared a moment later from the men's room. He grinned ear to ear. "Check this out. It's got pockets!"

My own smile froze. I wasn't sure what I expected. An emerald green velveteen jumpsuit was a whole lot of look. Probably not a look many guys intentionally went for. But unlike me, where my suit bunched and sagged in odd places, Ethan's fit snugly across his chest and shoulders and appeared to have an almost tailored fit. He wore that elf suit like a boss.

Ethan as a hot boss elf? *Yes, please.* A righthand man to Santa never looked so good. My cheeks flamed. How was it I found a Christmas elf so hot?

No. I found Ethan hot. Hot in the kitchen, and hot as an elf. I was done for.

"Come on. I don't look *that* bad do I?" He shifted his stance, causing the bells to jingle on his matching green boot covers.

"You look...great," I choked out. Did he understand the agony his sexy elf self caused me? We were here to serve children!

He winked at me. Winked! "Let's roll."

We joined the volunteers, including the hired Santa with a genuine white beard.

Santa looked directly at me. "Well, I know you."

"I've been good, I swear. Mostly." An unsteady laugh escaped. He couldn't tell by sight I was less than thrilled by his main gig holiday, could he?

He laughed in a jolly way. Holding his belly and everything. The man was *good*. "I'm honored to meet the famous Marlowe Holly in person. Your grandmother thinks the world of you."

Grans bragging on me?

"I know she's thrilled you're here visiting," he went on. "You're the one she always knew would do incredible and amazing things."

"Aw, Santa. You flatter me too much." Inside, my brain processed this information at hyperspeed. Grans kept her praise specific and task related. She wasn't one for big grand statements. I didn't doubt she'd thought those things, but to hear her supposed words from the mouth of a trusted Saint Nick? That hit different.

Grans always encouraged me to be me. It's why I knew I could leave in the first place. She and Gramps encouraged me to explore. They didn't hassle me to come home.

Maybe I wished they had. Maybe I had been running. Chasing after something I couldn't pin down.

Families began to arrive, and the tone shifted from my existential pondering to following directions. I came here to serve. As an elf in an emerald green jumpsuit.

As children's voices filled the room, and the elf suit urged my sweat glands into action, I looked into Ethan's eyes, and all was right in our little corner of the world.

"Marlowe." He moved in close. So close. "Your hat is a little too straight." He slid it to the side. "There. Perfect."

Chapter 18

Ethan

Bright and early the next day, I made my way to the tree farm. My thoughts buzzed with everything Marlowe.

I wanted to kiss her again. I wanted to kiss her every day. And I would have again last night, but the mood hadn't been right. She'd looked so stinking cute in that too-big elf suit, probably itching to ditch it. But she'd smiled and handed out presents like she'd been waiting for the opportunity all year.

Marlowe shined. As an *elf*. It was a sight to behold.

I could still hardly believe she'd kissed me. *She* had kissed *me*.

I'd never had the nerve to go for it with Marlowe. Even now, spending nearly every day together, I still hadn't made a move. But she had.

And then immediately freaked out.

I couldn't blame her. We didn't have a road map for this. No real idea where our lives would end up after the holidays.

I entered the outbuilding and stopped short at a man sitting in our office. "Dad? You're not supposed to be here."

He pointed to a bulky boot with Velcro straps on his foot. "Doc gave me this. I'm allowed to walk if I'm careful and don't put too much pressure on my ankle." He hoisted himself up from the kitchenette table and slowly made his way to his desk.

"Let me help." I gave him an assist to his chair at the desk. "Does Mom know you're here?"

"She drove me here, so that's likely a yes."

I crossed the room and shoved my lunch into the old refrigerator. "Anything you're doing here you can do from home. With the magic of technology."

"Son. Your mother wanted me out of the house. If you're going to lecture anybody, save it for her."

Ah. So more existed to this story. I would definitely not be lecturing Mom.

He gestured toward the empty chair in front of his desk, the one not piled with tattered notebooks and aging binders. "Sit down a minute. Tell me what you've been up to."

I sat and gave him a rundown of the past several days. Sales figures, small mishaps, and why the screen door leaned against the side of the building instead of hooked into its hinges.

Dad nodded along as he listened. "How about Marlowe? Jan Vasquez told me she saw you both running a table at the church bake sale. And my buddy Ken said she entered a cake in a competition. Marlowe? Baking?" Amusement glinted in his eye.

I winced. "It's nothing. I've been helping her with some things is all."

"I seem to recall her having the opposite of a green thumb in the kitchen. Or whatever the equivalent is for gardening when it involves a stove." He chuckled.

I hadn't told my parents about the Holly family's competition because of the secrecy surrounding the prize of the estate. My brother knew since he'd been there when Ashe told us, but Rob didn't care about town gossip, let alone care enough to spread it.

"Uh, yeah, Marlowe isn't much of a baker. Her grandmother wanted the whole family to do Holly Days' stuff, so she asked me for help."

"So you two baked a cake?" He seemed very interested in this development.

"Yeah. A fancy sponge cake. It turned out pretty great, actually, even though she didn't place."

Dad paused, considering. "She moving back here?"

I picked at the corner of the desk where the fake wood coating peeled away from the base. "I don't know. Probably not. Maybe? She has a lot going on."

"Heard any rumors of Emmaline selling?"

"The house?" I met his gaze. "Have you?" *Tread carefully.*

"I thought given you and Marlowe have been thick as thieves again, she might have said something. Figured Emmaline had something up her sleeve."

Dad nailed it, but I wasn't sure how much I could say about the house or the deal with Marlowe. But this was my own father. The Hollybrooke House land related to our business, to our family legacy. He'd been considering retirement seriously enough to tell his friends I might want a job at their construction business. I had to act.

I shifted forward on the vinyl chair. "You're not far off. Emmaline proposed a deal to her family. She called them all in because she wants to pass the house on to the next generation. It's a bit, uh, convoluted how it will all play out, to be honest."

He took a swig of coffee from a faded Sawyer Tree Farm mug. "I'll wait on Emmaline to bring it up then. She'll be asking after those extra acres."

That got my attention. "You know about the extra acres? For the deal?" Okay. Here I had another opportunity to lay out my plans and intentions. I had to convince him how serious I took the expansion idea. "That's what I'm hoping for. Whoever gets the house—and it may be Marlowe because she's aiming for it—then we buy off a few acres for the expansion. The business plan I showed you, we can increase our growth and convert the barn into a gift shop. Build a new outbuilding. We need the space. I'm willing to take on the work and negotiate a deal."

My dad returned a puzzled expression. "I'm not talking about *more* acres. I meant the ones we already use from the Hollys."

Now I was the one puzzled. "I don't understand."

"The spot where the old fence remnant stands? In the west corner? That's the end of our property."

I shook my head. "No, our property line extends to the chain fence."

"Huh. I figured you knew. That's Holly property. Emmaline's late husband gave it to us in a, I'll say, gentleman's agreement. There's no paperwork for it. He just said if I needed the extra couple acres, go ahead and use 'em."

My body grew still. I spoke with cautious words. "Dad, are you suggesting—"

He cleared his throat. "I'm not suggesting anything. We don't own those three acres. That's officially Holly property. And they can take that back whenever the whim strikes."

"Holly Days Teams, assemble!" Mayor Bennington announced from the small stage in Crystal Cove's town square. It seemed like the whole town showed up today. The Holly family gathered in small groups by family, ready for action at the Holly Days' Family Fest competition.

I arrived somewhere between fuming and amped up. Like a triathlete ready to...try-athlete.

I still couldn't shake off the news Dad casually dropped yesterday. Not only did the Sawyer farm require more land in order to expand, we needed an official deed signed for the land we were *already using.* If we lost those three acres, we were toast. My whole plan to expand the farm would be pointless.

I had no idea if any of the other Hollys would honor the agreement Dad had made with Marlowe's grandfather. Let alone allow us to buy more land. We sure couldn't afford to lose what we had. Tree farms over the border in Wisconsin would gladly set up shop in town in place of us once they knew we were downsizing. Or closing altogether.

Marlowe had no idea. I didn't like keeping secrets between us, but this new information risked a lot for me. If she questioned her family on it, she could accidentally expose our plan. Besides, if I told her, she might assume us getting closer was some ploy just to get the land. I'd kissed her because I wanted to. I'd always wanted to. I couldn't let her believe I was using her. No, it made the most sense to keep this quiet for now. Take this all one day at a time.

What we needed was to win this dang competition.

"The obstacle race will be a piece of cake." Marlowe appeared oblivious to my inner stewing. "And thankfully, no actual cake is involved. I am so tired of baking."

"Good thing since we bought ten pounds of gingerbread ingredients." The fate of my family's farm rested on obstacle courses and candy houses. Unbelievable.

"Sure, sure." Marlowe flit a hand in the air. "A physical competition is great. We have an edge. The main thing I do for fun outside of work is working out."

"That still has the word *work* in it."

"Okay, exercising. Fitness."

"Fitness for fun?" I scrunched my face to get a reaction out of her. She swatted me. *Score.*

"You're fit. You're telling me you don't work out?" She pressed her gloved hand against my upper arm. She made a low murmur as she ran her hand along the muscle. "You're sturdy, Sawyer."

She had no idea what she was doing to me. My body ran hot already, and I'd be steaming before too long. "I do farm work. I don't exactly need a bicycling class to stay in shape." Never mind the part where I lifted free weights in my apartment living room.

"You mean spinning class?" She grinned at me. "Regardless, it's impressive."

Me—impressive. Marlowe Holly thought me—my body—was impressive. If high school me could time travel and see this moment, maybe I wouldn't have been so mopey over her junior and senior year.

This was pure torture, in the best way. It took everything I had not to kiss her again. Heck, *she'd kissed me.* But I wasn't stupid. In her own time, she'd let me know if she was ready for more. And in my own time, I'd tell her about our unofficial land use.

At the moment, I needed to focus. We needed to score big points today. Points, land, farm. Those were my goals.

A team could mean any arrangement of contestants, so ours included two friends I'd recruited for the weekend. Here they were now, right on time.

"Marlowe, this is Megan and you know Nick already. Nick Bennington. They're visiting from Chicago."

Nick, tall like me but more broad shouldered, looked like the lead in one of those holiday romance movies. He'd be the one cast to work at the tree farm in the movie version of my life. And he'd already won over the city girl too. He just became a city guy instead of sticking around the small town.

Nick gestured to Marlowe. "Marlowe Holly? I haven't seen you since high school graduation."

"Hey, Nick. Nice to see you." Her cheeks colored at the attention. Or maybe it was the brisk air. "To be clear, we're here to beat the stuffing out of my family."

He nodded. "Understood."

"Oh, you're a Holly?" Megan asked. She wore a knit cap with a fuzzy ball on top and winter clothes fresh from an outdoor gear store. Her pale skin looked like she stayed away from harsh weather elements. "My parents talk about the Holly family like they run this town." She jabbed Nick with her elbow. "The Hollys might even be more popular than the Benningtons."

"Don't remind me." Marlowe laughed, but the sound came strained.

"We all have family identities to outgrow, right?" I offered.

Marlowe winced. Megan bit her lip, looking between us. Nick jogged in place, oblivious or ignoring the tension. I admired his commitment.

"Nick's mom is the mayor," I filled in for Marlowe's sake.

Her eyes lit with understanding. "Oh. I didn't realize. Or remember. I mean, she wasn't mayor when I last lived here."

"I managed to offend Nick's mom and half the town at a charity event last year." Megan tugged down the sides of her knit cap. "I had my own family stuff going on and blurted out something so clueless. Anyway, I'm here to rock this competition." She held up her fist for a bump and Marlowe met the request.

The tense vibe disappeared. "Awesome. Same."

A whistle blew and we were directed to the obstacle course, which included physical challenges like a tire run and a short climbing wall.

Marlowe squinted into the distance. "Is that a Christmas tree? On an obstacle course?"

"It's Holly Days," I reminded her. "Everything has a holiday twist." She growled.

"It's cute," Megan said. "It looks like there's a box of decorations next to each tree. So we have to decorate it before we move on to the next obstacle."

"Listen up," a bald Black man wearing a Holly Days Family Fest Crew vest announced. "The team splits for each obstacle run. Tag off when you complete your leg of the race."

"I am *not* decorating a tree," Marlowe announced. She cleared her throat. "Um, that sounded incredibly humbug of me. I would prefer the tire run and the climbing wall."

"Aw, did you call yourself a humbug?" Megan laughed.

"Recovering humbug," I suggested. "We're working on it."

Marlowe held her chin high. "I listened to a whole song about eggnog and roasting chestnuts on the way over. The whole thing."

The whistle blew again. "Get ready to start in three, two, one—go!"

The day progressed with exhausting but fun activities. Marlowe gave the event her full attention and physical effort. Seeing her happy took my mind off pressing worries—those unsecured acres, my dad, and my own uncertain future.

By my count, Rafe and Brianne and their athletic kids led in today's family bracket of points. Riley and her daughter had two other fit adults with them, but I counted them behind in points from Shawn and Ashe, who'd teamed up today with Ashe's oldest two kids.

"How's that working with your brothers on the same team today?" I asked Marlowe. The family contest rules were confounding at times. Rafe and Riley had shared any activity but not others. Now her brothers.

"Yeah, I noticed that too, but TL approved it." She popped a marshmallow into her mouth. We sat at a long table in the same tent used for the Tasty Bake competition last weekend, with added space heaters to keep the temperature up. "I can't believe we're building snow people out of marshmallows." She examined her lumpy, unsteady sugar creation. "At least it doesn't involve an oven."

"A few years ago, the town moved the snowman building contest to late January when we almost always have snow," I told her. "December is a wild card for weather. They kept having to cancel the event."

If I was smart, I'd head back to the farm. Rob assured me he had things covered. We'd already lost sales when the tree lot by the highway closed early for staffing two nights this week. Our seasonal staff this year weren't exactly dependable. One guy I had to fire. His girlfriend surprised him with Chicago Bears tickets which for him trumped standing in the cold parking lot selling trees. He texted us his "cancellation of shift" on the way to the game. An hour *after* the start time for his shift.

Beside me, Marlowe worked quietly to construct her snow being. We were basically doing little kids' crafts, which was all fine and good for a family festival, but I had questions when land rights were on the line. "Back to the teams and the points. Are Ashe and Shawn splitting today's points somehow?"

"I don't understand the points system. I think Grans just wants us all here together."

Sure enough, Emmaline Holly sat in a center seat with the Holly generations surrounding her. She laughed as Reece attempted to walk her marshmallow robot off its paper plate base. Marlowe's aunt Sunny snapped photos of her own grandkids, Rafe and Riley's kids, and seemed the least stressed of anybody, given she and Marlowe's uncle weren't in the running to win the house.

My neck began to sweat. "Okay sure, your family is doing family stuff." I lowered my voice. "Our arrangement is a big deal to me. I need to know if we can actually win this thing."

Marlowe blew out a breath of frustration. "I don't make the rules. I don't know."

She was acting awfully aloof about this.

"Your life stands to change a pretty big amount if you win. Aren't you concerned how this is all adding up?" I looked at my own paper plate with a pile of loose candy and marshmallows. "This competition is a *joke*."

Marlowe's expression shifted. She angled her body away from her family to close us in. "When it comes down to it, Grans will give the house to whoever deserves it. *I* deserve it. I have a plan and I'm not wavering."

"A plan besides the competition?" My thoughts raced. "Is there something you're not telling me? We're in this together. I need to know details."

Never mind I hadn't told her about those extra borrowed acres. I couldn't tell her here. Not with so many people around.

"That's not even anything," a droll voice sounded over my shoulder.

TL, the goth teen who would determine our future, turned her nose up at my pile of candy.

The chatter buzzing around us drained my ability to think straight. Marlowe wasn't hearing me. She wasn't seeing how much I—we—stood to lose.

I shoved the plate aside and zeroed in on Marlowe. "We need to talk. About the competition and these points. I'm all for a fun day out with the family, but none of this makes any sense. The points mean nothing. I can't believe someone will win the Hollybrooke House for making a craft out of a marshmallow!"

Something weird was happening. Or not happening, more like. The talking around us stopped. The tent grew eerily quiet. The Holly family, including Emmaline, stared at me. Daggers from Emmaline, and swords and other spears from Marlowe's brothers and cousins.

TL shrugged and moved on.

Marlowe herself simply sighed. "This doesn't bode well."

Chapter 19

Marlowe

"Did I just hear you're looking to offload the Hollybrooke property?" Arlene, who helped judge the bake sale and served as oversight for our current activity, approached Grans at the marshmallow building table with the family. Her question boomed across the tent.

How did Arlene project her voice so loud? Oh, right. Because she had a microphone clipped to her coat collar. Arlene spoke into a hot mic.

"I didn't know you were moving, Emmaline," Mr. Kowalczyk from the post office called out.

A judge from the book club gasped. "Are you passing down the Holly house? Is winning the house part of the contest?"

"As a judge in this competition, I am not aware of any prizes involving the sale of the Hollybrooke estate," Arlene spoke into her very hot, live, microphone. "Emmaline? What is this about?"

The chatter inside the tent grew louder. Grans remained composed aside from a single finger pressed against her temple. No one outside the family should have known the stakes—not even her panel of judges. They were told this contest was simply Grans orchestrating an elaborate new family tradition.

I looked at Ethan. His face reddened. "I'm sorry, I didn't mean—"

"You know what? You're right. All of this is ridiculous."

Ethan held his hands in a gesture of surrender. "I said it was a joke, not ridiculous." He lowered his hands. "Right. That doesn't sound any better."

Shawn pointed a menacing finger at Ethan. "You better not ruin this for me."

"Stop pointing at him," I shot back to my brother. "You are perfectly capable of ruining things all by yourself."

He shifted his pointing finger at me. "I have the best business sense of any of us. I'll take care of the house and keep it in the family. The way it should be."

Rafe snorted. "I work for an international company and negotiate sales deals every day. My wife is an office manager and sits on the board of four organizations. You don't think we have business sense?"

Shawn shrugged. "Sure. I'm just sayin' mine is better."

Rafe stood at his end of the table. "We deserve this house and we're ready to prove it. By my accounting, my family is in the lead."

Ashe bolted to his feet, causing his metal folding chair to tip. "No, *we're* winning. Shawn and I caught up today with our points split strategy."

"I knew something was up with them," Ethan muttered.

"Say it to my face, Sawyer." Shawn closed the space between them and shadowed over Ethan, still seated.

Ethan sprung from his chair. He had several inches in height over my suddenly menacing brother. "I knew your point sharing with Ashe was shady." He looked past Shawn to Ashe. "Yeah, I said it. You two are acting *shady*."

I broke in between Shawn and Ethan before the testosterone boiled over.

Too late. Testosterone sizzled against the burner flames. This tent escalated to piping hot like that microphone. Ashe barreled past me. "Let's take this outside. Right now."

They took it outside. The guys, muttering and sniping at each other, followed Ashe, their head tantruming adult, as he stomped from the tent into the town square.

I dashed out behind them along with Brianne, Riley, and a swarm of kids. Half the tent emptied out with us. The square bustled with shoppers at the holiday haus shops and food vendors.

Ashe, Shawn, Ethan, and Rafe stood in a circle and spoke in escalating voices at each other. Snippets carried over about who deserved the house, things not being fair, and something about a broken bike in fifth grade. A scolding Brianne tugged Rafe back, leaving an opening for Riley to slide in and join the bickering. The *loud* bickering.

This was not a good look for the Holly family.

Apparently, snow had started falling while we'd been inside the tent. A soft dusting coated the ground and wide, fluffy flakes fluttered down. Early winter snow set the scene like a snow globe, except for the squabbling family stationed at the center.

A little girl tugged on my sleeve. "Are they going to brawl?"

I gaped at her. I wanted to say no. Surely, my family knew better than this. Surely, Ethan knew better.

Shawn bent down and mashed a wad of snow together. He flung it at Ethan. "Here's your snowman contest right here."

The snow instantly broke apart and hit Ethan's chest in light, scattered glops. There wasn't enough of it to form a decent snowball. Ethan stood still. Looked down at his wet shirt, then back at Shawn.

Without a word, they tackled each other at the same time.

"No!" I broke through the crowd. I had to do something.

Ashe attempted to pull Shawn back, but the guys had fallen to the ground and wrestled in the snow. Ashe didn't see it coming when Rafe smacked a hand full of wet snow against the back of his neck. "Ah—that's cold!"

"Get him, Dad!" Rafe's kids squealed.

I inched forward, unsure what to do other than to yell at them to stop.

TL appeared beside me. "What an embarrassing display of male rage." She held up her phone, recording.

Great, just great.

"My mom's there too," Reece told TL. "The guys always take credit for everything. Look—my mom shoved Uncle Rafe. Did you record that?" She sounded proud.

"Fighting isn't something to brag about," I said to Reece.

Ethan and Shawn were on their feet now. Both ran at Rafe. Ashe followed. Something had shifted—I must have missed it with my sad attempt at a lecture.

They raced across the square. Why? For what purpose?

"They're headed for the display!" Arlene cried out. Still with the mic on, amplified in the tent, but audible outside in the square.

Sure enough, they ran toward the big Christmas tree in the center of the square with its surrounding holiday decorations.

An elderly white man peered past me. "I can't see. Arlene, tell us what's happening."

Arlene switched her voice to the tone of a sports announcer. "We've got Rafe Holly in the lead with Shawn Holly hot on his heels. Don't count out the Sawyer boy making strides or Ashe Holly coming up on the left. Rafe will need to pivot fast if he wants to avoid—oh! There goes the Menorah."

I winced as the ten-foot-tall Menorah tipped over. Thankfully, it was inflatable.

A high-pitched squeak sounded. It was coming from the Menorah. They'd punctured the Menorah.

The crowd gasped and inched forward to ogle the chaos.

"Shawn Holly hits the ground tackled by brother Ashe," Arlene continued to narrate, having now unclipped the mic from her lapel to hold it close to her mouth. "Ashe played running back for Crystal Cove High and made division all-state two years running."

Light chatter surfaced among the crowd about Crystal Cove's current football stats.

This was obnoxious. Someone would get hurt. I advanced toward the display, hoping I could talk sense into them. "Stop embarrassing us, you dummies!" I shouted to unhearing ears.

Shawn rolled out of Ashe's reach and stumbled to his feet. Ashe, attempting to stand, caught his foot on the edge of a hay bale bordering the display manager. He fell backward and knocked over a wise man. At least there were two wise men left standing, which sure didn't include my brother.

Shawn pointed at Ashe and cackled. "Told ya you couldn't catch me."

Seriously? Two grown men playing chase? In a public square?

I wouldn't call Ashe quick to anger. Even with three kids, he had the patience of twelve church ladies on bake sale day. When Ashe got mad—really mad—he got quiet. And still.

Ashe ceased all movement. He did not speak. His glare toward Shawn could be seen from space.

He flipped to all fours and scuttled around. "You better run," he ground out.

Shawn's smirk faded. Actual fear lit his eyes. He turned to bolt just as Ashe scrambled up and reached for something.

Oh...oh no.

"He's got the baby Jesus," Arlene gasped into her microphone. "I repeat, Ashe Holly is in possession of the baby Jesus!"

No. Do not throw the baby Jesus. "ASHE!" I screamed at him. What was he thinking? Where was his wife? She was probably drowning her sorrows in spiked hot chocolate somewhere because she had more sense than the rest of us.

Ashe, with the blanketed baby Jesus piece from the display manger, cradled the bundle like a football. He arched back his arm.

"And here comes Ethan Sawyer," Arlene's commentary cut in. "A tackle to the ground!"

But not before Ashe launched baby Jesus into the air.

We would never live this down. Never.

Out of nowhere, Tyler, Ashe's oldest son, sprinted from the sidelines and caught the baby bundle.

"Interception!" Arlene called out. "Baby Jesus has been intercepted—it's a miracle!" She cleared her throat. "Please return the display baby to its cradle."

Crisis averted? I glanced around. Half the gawkers pointed their phones toward my family causing havoc. Nope, we would not live this down.

"I knew we should have secured the baby."

I turned, horrified. Nick's mom, Mrs. Bennington—make that Mayor Bennington—scowled, but I could have sworn her eyes danced with amusement.

Suddenly, a voice boomed louder than the crowd noise. "ENOUGH!"

A stoic matriarch parted the crowd and advanced like a queen whose succession had been questioned. "Absolutely *enough* of this hooliganry." Grans' words scorched like steel still smoldering from the forge. "All of you return to the house. *Immediately*."

Chapter 20

Marlowe

Tension circulated in Murdoch on the ride to Hollybrooke House with Ethan. I'd made such a mess of things. Well, my brothers and cousin had made a literal mess.

I'd planned on apologizing to Ethan for involving him in such a circus. Then all things circus broke loose. Merely short a few monkeys or we could have sold tickets. "You guys deflated the town Menorah." It was still shocking. "And don't get me started on baby Jesus."

Ethan winced. "Look, I'm sorry." He stared out the window. "I don't know what got into me. Something activated when Shawn got in my face."

"He has that effect on people." We drove past familiar town landmarks. The public library, the Presbyterian church facing the Catholic church across the street from it, the strip mall that used to house a dry cleaner and a dance studio, now a chain dollar store, same as the one by my apartment in San Jose. "I wanted to apologize myself. For all of it. This is all really, really weird."

Ethan knocked his knuckles absently on the passenger side window. "Your family loves you. Your grandmother was desperate to see you all together again. We both got swept up in this—I got swept up in the idea we could win."

"No. There is no sweeping involved. No brooms to speak of. This obnoxious Holly Games Caper is my family at peak weirdness. It's an *embarrassment*. I'm sorry I involved you."

I'd always been proud of my family. Obviously, some people thought we were strange, or the opposite of normal, whatever that meant. But this? The whole contest and the fighting in town square proved we were beyond *extra* and more like a dump truck of *too much*.

"They're not embarrassing," Ethan said quietly. "Today's...situation aside. I'm glad I've been a part of it the past few weeks because it brought us together. Even if I'm frustrated by what's happening. *Incredibly* frustrated."

My chest grew tight. I'd roped Ethan into this competition, pretending to date him in front of my family, and for what? What would I do with a whole, huge Victorian house in a town I wasn't sure I wanted to live in once the holidays ended?

And Ethan. Our time together hadn't been solely about winning a house. Who was I kidding? That first night back at Checkers my long buried feelings already began clawing back to the surface. Getting my feelings tied up with this contest was the last thing I'd expected. Getting *his* feelings tied up with mine, well that simply wasn't fair to Ethan at all.

Once he didn't need to spend time with me, why would he? I'd used him. If we lost the house, I'd lose him too.

Losing the house came at a cost to Ethan. He had a legitimate family business, which was in crisis, or would be if he couldn't get what he needed. Here he was putting up with marshmallow crafts. Naturally, he'd lost it. I wouldn't defend his physically fighting with my brothers, but I could see how his frustration hit its limit.

"I'll be lucky to get a bank loan with that video footage floating around," Ethan grumbled. "I'd hoped our family's good reputation would help with the local bank, but now?" He laughed without humor.

Mild panic set in. "You don't know they'll reject you. We can save this. We still have a chance if we let Grans know how sorry we are—"

Ethan's sigh cut my words short. "I don't know, Marlowe."

We needed to talk. Really talk. I couldn't continue counting on distractions.

I slowed and angled into the parking lot of The Dairy Freeze, now shuttered for the season. I parked but kept Murdoch idling for heat. I needed a beat to breathe, which Ethan didn't question. Almost like he anticipated the detour.

So I breathed. The day's dramatics cycled through my mind. So many questions with few answers. Running beneath the surface was what I'd been avoiding for days. Weeks. Years?

"You were never freaked out by me having dead parents." The words burst out of me. "Why?"

Ethan freed himself from the seatbelt and hunched forward with his elbows at his knees. "You had a great family. Why would I be freaked out?"

I could never understand it either. And yet, the pitying looks, the outright avoidance by girls at school. The piqued interest in high school by the outcast kids, many who had troubling home situations. I never felt troubled, but it was as if people were suggesting there was something wrong with me that I wasn't. "You saw me as Marlowe. Not as a Holly. I was just...your friend."

Ethan watched me. "And now?"

Jangly holiday music played at a low volume from the car stereo. Now? We were fake dating to win a kooky competition for pretty big stakes. Now we'd altered a lifetime of friendship with a kiss. I wasn't sure where to go from here. But I needed to face this. "I'm glad you're here, Ethan. At the same time, I regret involving you at all."

He angled toward me. "I don't regret anything with you, Marlowe."

My heart triple flipped and landed deep in my chest. It stuck the landing until he spoke again.

"Okay, I regret one thing." He spoke at the window and fidgeted with a metallic piece of ribbon probably leftover from today's crafts. "See, I care about you. I *have* cared about you. For a long time. I never told you how much. I regret not telling you how much."

Love isn't conditional. He'd told me as much at the farm.

Love. *Love* wasn't conditional.

"Ethan, do you mean..." I wanted him to say it. Out loud. "Wait." Maybe he needed to hear it from me. I'd been the one to hold back so long when Ethan had always been there. He had, right? Always been there? Waiting...on me.

"I also...care." I squeezed my eyes shut at my own awkwardness. Why was this so hard? Ethan could be anywhere right now, including working at his own business, and yet he sat here in an aging town car driven by a woman whose family orchestrated elaborate (and festive) obstacles for their own amusement.

A woman who loved him.

The realization shook me. *I loved Ethan.* Not simply a crush or a nostalgic memory. I loved Ethan now. For the man he'd become. For who he strived to be. And all of the in between.

I'd always loved Ethan. It was almost unimaginable to think otherwise. I wasn't sure what understanding this love meant for us, but I knew it was the truth. And he deserved to know.

Everything else fell away. Ethan looked up and centered his focus on me. Looking. Not staring, but looking. Waiting.

"Why are you looking at me?" I asked, barely above a whisper.

"Because you're beautiful."

He said it so simply.

"Ethan, I—"

He silenced my confession with his lips.

My mind flooded with memories. Ethan's smile. Running through the property to the boundary fence by his farm. Building tree forts, hours of video games, secret bike paths. School dances where we lurked by the snack table. Baking together last week. Our kiss on the couch.

This kiss felt hopelessly late and right on time.

His fingers trailed against my cheek. Next, they made a slow climb into my hair. Starting from the nape of my neck, traveling to cradle the back of my head. Teasing my hair as he teased me with soft lips.

Why hadn't we been doing this for weeks? Years?

I angled to taste him better. I needed to show Ethan how much I wanted this. Us. Together. We'd figure out the rest.

Heat spread through my body. This was new and so familiar. Like I'd come home.

Home. I was home. I sensed it, finally, to my roots. It wasn't the place but the people. It was him. Home was Ethan.

The kiss deepened and nearly melted me like a real non-marshmallow snow lady. Warmth ignited my senses and settled like a wash of comfort. Peace and excitement all at once. We parted.

My head spun close to the clouds. "I'm in love with you. And I have been for a very long time."

Those were my words. I'd said them out loud, to a completely shocked Ethan Sawyer.

Chapter 21

Ethan

She loves me. Marlowe said she was *in love* with me.

"For a…very long time?" I managed to ask.

She nodded.

Marlowe loved me. Going back years. How had I missed it? How had *we* missed saying these key words when we'd both been so gone for each other?

"I can't remember a time not loving you," I told her.

She pulled at my shirt collar—a nearly desperate pull—until our lips found each other. Showing me she understood with kiss after kiss.

When we parted, she came up breathless. "I never wanted to ruin our friendship. I was terrified of messing up what we had. Then I ended up ruining it anyway by distancing from you. I felt so out of whack in high school. So messy. Like I needed space but I couldn't go anywhere. When I had the space, it's like I went too far the other direction. I was…scared to come back, I think."

What she said made sense. So much sense.

I kissed her again, with everything I had. She needed to know I didn't care about being messy or needing space. We both had our own stuff to work through. The point being, we could deal with it together.

She shifted closer. I wasn't sure how since we were nearly on top of each other in the front seat. All the times I'd imagined moments like this with Marlowe and it was happening right now.

When I eased back, she made a quiet sound of protest. I could barely speak I felt so amped. "Let's not give up."

A dreamy look struck her face. "Yeah. Never." Her lips glided across mine, sealing in the sense we were onto something here.

I nodded. "We can still win the land and the house."

The radio suddenly blared a commercial at an obnoxious decibel. We shot apart as if the airwaves wedged hands between us like an invisible chaperone.

Marlowe twisted forward again in the driver's seat. "Right. The house." Her eyebrows flew up. "Oh my gosh—the family meeting. Buckle up. We need to go."

We arrived late in a tangle to the Holly family meeting. Klutzy and laughing, we tripped over scattered boots and children's shoes in the mudroom. Marlowe's hair struck wild poses, and my coat lay abandoned in Murdoch. We looked like two kids who, as my granddad would say, had been necking in the car.

What did that mean anyway? Literally *necks* touching?

Because our necks had definitely touched. Our lips, our breaths, our hands. Like we'd reached the summit of a gradual incline we'd traveled most of our lives. Through childhood silliness to shifting degrees of friendship to whatever this new thing was between us.

Marlowe peeled off her coat and led me by the hand down the hall. How could I face the rest of the Holly brood like this? One thing took up my brain space. A phrase running constant like the background sounds of WKCC holiday radio. *I'm in love with you.*

I didn't expect the impact. I'd convinced myself Marlowe existed as a happy memory. A high school crush I couldn't get over and probably needed to actually get over.

Right now, I didn't care. We landed in the doorway to the family room. Marlowe held my hand and we presented a united front to her family.

Ashe made a face. "Look who decided to show up. We've all been waiting while you two couldn't keep your hands off each other."

"Told ya," Shawn sneered at Ashe. "Also, I knew they were together before any of you did."

"Come on, it was obvious the minute we walked into Checkers," said Ashe. "I knew before you could form a coherent thought."

Marlowe's cheeks flushed like their namesake berry. "Sorry we're late. We...hit traffic."

Rafe sneered. "Behind what, a tractor going twenty miles an hour?"

Marlowe shifted beside me. She didn't bother glaring at her cousin. She must really be flustered. "It's my fault," I said.

"I bet it was," Ashe muttered. "Like starting a fight in front of everybody in town."

Okay, no way. No freaking way. "I'll take blame for spilling the beans about the competition for the house—that's on me. But I would never, ever go for a long pass with the town's Holy Child."

Ashe tossed out an exaggerated shrug. "They should've bolted the baby down if they wanted it secured."

Emmaline entered the room and crossed in front of us to her chair by the window. "Every single one of you should be ashamed of the spectacle you caused today." Her crisp tone closed the door on the chatter. "Ethan Sawyer, have a seat."

I blinked, realizing Marlowe had unattached her hand and found a vacant spot on a footstool. The only remaining open space waited on the couch beside Ashe, Cara, and their youngest who stretched out with feet planted on his mom's lap playing games on a tablet. I took the floor by Marlowe.

"There are dogs better behaved than you all." Emmaline returned a disapproving frown. "I told Mayor Bennington to expect handwritten apologies from each of you, as well as a commitment to pick up road trash by the highway. I asked for the least desirable volunteer work available. For the record, she offered shifts at the animal shelter and I told her no."

I'd never seen Emmaline Holly so angry.

She observed us from her corner chair. "I've seen time and again how wills and inheritances fracture families. I thought the Holly family was above such foolishness. I believed we could spare any future turmoil by handling the estate now. And to think, if I'd waited, you'd all be at each other's throats at my funeral."

A half dozen dog tails lowered in shame.

She'd made the inheritance a contest. Of course it would get competitive. Possibly petty. I wanted to ask her what she'd expected. But no way would I say that out loud.

Emmaline sighed. "The secret is out about the house."

The stares of a dozen Hollys descended on me. "Sorry." I straightened and looked at the Holly matriarch directly. "I'm sorry, ma'am."

She nodded in one curt motion. "It was unrealistic to expect I could keep my plans to leave hidden. I'm questioned about the house nearly every time I go into town. When I showed interest to Paulette Hart about the new retirement community at the seniors' expo, I knew I'd made a crucial mistake. I've had to fend off rumors about selling for months."

While it sounded dramatic, lots of folks around here traded gossip like currency. Town "news" was the second most popular conversation starter after the weather. And people always speculated about the Holly house, especially after Emmaline's husband passed. Some went as far as saying she was selfish for living in such a big house all by herself, despite her grandkids and their families frequently visiting and using the home for holidays and family parties.

Emmaline gave a light shrug. "The gossips I can handle. My goal is to protect the family estate from vultures aiming to dice up our property to the highest bidder."

I didn't dare move or make a sound. Did she know my family already farmed on Holly land? Dad implied she'd be asking about it. What would happen now? If I hadn't blown up at Shawn, maybe none of this would have happened and we'd be celebrating a marshmallow contest victory. Yeah right—I'd already given up on the marshmallows.

I could only blame myself for putting stock in this idea in the first place.

Riley shook her head with impatience. "Isn't that what Shawn would do anyway? Sell the land?"

"I never said I'd *actually* sell it," he countered.

"Selling properties is your job," Rafe shot back. "Number three in the Tallahassee market, right?"

Bickering commenced with raised voices.

"*Stop.*" Emmaline's own raised voice settled the room again. "The idea of bringing the family together for a holiday competition felt so exhilarating and, well, whimsical. One last hurrah before life changed yet again and this house no longer belonged to me. I severely underestimated your devotion to this home."

Her gaze landed on Marlowe, who stared at her hands.

"So is the competition called off?" Cara asked. I didn't miss the hopeful note in her question.

"Called off—I'm in the lead!" Rafe exclaimed.

Shawn pointed at Rafe. "No, *I* am."

"I'd like a re-tally of all points," Marlowe stated in a clear, strong voice. She nudged me with her foot.

The points were a mess. We needed to *do* something.

Riley and Shawn argued while Cara grumbled unintelligibly to Ashe.

Rafe jumped to his feet and paced by the bay window. "Let's be logical here. I've played along with this competition for Grans' sake, but it's time to stop playing games. The path to inheritance is clear as crystal. The house should pass to me, as I'm the eldest child of the next living generation."

The air sucked out of the room. The phrase *living generation* pulsed like a beacon. By Rafe's logic, Marlowe, Shawn, and Ashe weren't in line for inheritance because they lacked a living generation between them and Emmaline.

The exact thing Marlowe complained people defined her for, and this came from within her own family.

"Rafe," Brianne chided.

But it was too late. The room exploded. Marlowe bolted up at the same time as Ashe, declaring they had as much right to the Holly estate as him. Shawn picked a fight with Rafe by inviting him to step outside and solve this like men. Riley blamed Rafe for ruining the competition for all of them.

I got to my feet and stood behind Marlowe. I laid a hand at her back and she leaned into it, her emotions still flaring.

Rafe ignored Shawn and jeered our direction. "You don't need this house, Marlowe. It's a joke you're even here pretending at this 'lost high school crush' to gain Grans' attention."

"Come on, look at them," Cara called out. "They're surgically attached at this point. That's a lot of effort to fake."

Our dating *had* been a ruse, but now? Now things were different. She loved me. I loved her. We couldn't turn back now.

Riley scowled at her brother. "They've had a thing for each other since high school. It was totally obvious every time I was around them."

Oh, totally obvious, was it? Obvious to everyone but us.

"You only want the house to take it from the rest of us," Rafe continued. "You were always dead set on leaving this town. You barely bother visiting. You created your own happy Holly-less existence two thousand miles from here. So go back to your little California utopia and leave the estate planning to the adults in the room."

Adrenaline fueled me forward. "Marlowe *is* an adult. Start treating her like one. She has as much right to this home as any of you. And besides, she doesn't even have a—" I stopped myself just in time. Nope—said too much. I was no good at secret keeping. "Sorry, sorry," I muttered to Marlowe.

"She doesn't what?" Rafe hooked in, knowing I'd nearly spilled more precious details.

Marlowe held her chin up. "I'm no longer employed. I was laid off from my company prior to coming here."

The room quieted.

"Why didn't you tell us?" Ashe asked with notable hurt.

"Because obviously she enjoys lying," Rafe answered for her.

Marlowe fought against a quivering lip. "Because..." She gestured around the room. "Because of this. You still see me as the baby. You think I don't care because I dared to leave the nest. It doesn't mean I don't care. I had to leave for them. For *them*." She pointed to the portrait behind her where her parents smiled, frozen in time. "I had to show them I could do more than simply *exist* without them. I had to be more than just another Holly."

Rafe scoffed. "If you think that lowly of us, you don't deserve the house at all."

Shawn shoved a menacing pointer finger in Rafe's face. "Don't you insult my sister. That's *my* job."

Finally, Emmaline stood. She raised her hands like a conductor who'd lost control of an off-tune orchestra. "*Silence.*"

Emmaline looked down her nose at her legacy of bickering grandchildren. "You've forced my hand." She paced a small stretch of the room before speaking again. "*I* will decide who inherits this home. By Christmas Eve, I'll have an answer." She let her words sit as we all scrambled to catch up. "And before anyone leaves this room, you are all expected at caroling. The caroling is *mandatory*."

Chapter 22

Marlowe

I couldn't look Ethan in the eye. His face had paled when Grans declared she would determine the winner. He'd witnessed my family unravel over basic property rights. I'd promised him a fighting chance at the land, and now the likelihood of that happening had drastically reduced. All after I'd declared my love for him.

Would Ethan have ever agreed to be with me if the land hadn't been part of the package? It was a pretty sweet package, if I had any control over delivery.

And now my family knew my failures. Fancy Marlowe with her West Coast life no longer shined like a star. The supposed career I'd thrown myself into at the cost of losing touch with my family, gone. Now returned to my rightful spot as the family baby, they'd put me in my place.

If I was honest with myself, I had no business inheriting the house. I was just the last to realize it.

Sure, I could move home, but none of my family would ever take me seriously. To them, the idea of me inheriting the Hollybrooke House had been a punchline. To a pretty unfunny joke, if you asked me.

"Marlowe—" Ethan started.

I shook my head, willing my voice to remain calm. "I'm sorry. I'm so sorry..." For leading him into this deal. For promising too much. For letting myself dream of more. "Maybe you should go."

Ethan returned a neutral expression. Was he hurt? Shocked? Worried? I couldn't decipher. He certainly wasn't shaking with rage. "How about I'll text you later."

Texting, just like old times. Just like our new times. Back to usual.

No. We couldn't go back to usual. We'd risked our actual feelings and emotions in this ludicrous arrangement, not thinking whether we'd fail. I should give him an easy out. When the house and land went to another Holly, I couldn't imagine he'd want to stick around.

"Why bother?" I ground out. "It's not like there's any competition left."

His eyes softened. "You need space. I get it."

My chest ached. I didn't want him to go, but this was too humiliating. I didn't fit here. I'd ruined his plans. I needed ten minutes of dark solace in my closet and then I could regroup and properly freak out for real.

Ethan walked toward the door. I waited for him to turn around. To close the gap between us in two big, determined steps and sweep me off my feet. To say this whole thing would be a tiny blip in our memories someday. To say to heck with the house and the land and our families. Only *we* mattered. Us. Together.

But he didn't say those things and he didn't turn back. Without another word, Ethan left, just as I'd asked. I watched him from the bay window as he crossed the backyard, down the hill, and out to the tree farm in the distance.

The mood remained sour when we showed up to the town square warmly bundled for a night of caroling. It was ridiculous to think any of us could spread vocal holiday cheer in this state of mind.

Honestly, I was surprised we were allowed in. No gates closed off the square but our family had real nerve showing up after knocking down revered religious iconography. Inflatable or not.

The family mingled in separate groups, keeping to themselves. I hung out with the children, which cemented my place at the proverbial kids' table.

Grans hadn't arrived yet. This was her whole deal and she couldn't be bothered to show up on time. Even Uncle Joe and Aunt Sunny made their appearance with bells on. They wore actual jingle bells around their necks. And to think, I'd been close to maybe actually not hating Christmas. Even with snow gently dusting the ground and delicately clinging to tree branches, I couldn't muster any holiday joy.

Rafe scoffed loudly. "What's *he* doing here?"

Ethan appeared beside me. "Supporting my girlfriend."

I did a double take. Literally, I looked away and back again. His physical body did not disappear. "You don't have to pretend anymore."

Ethan didn't flinch. "Unless you tell me right now you want me to leave, and that what has happened between us meant nothing, I'm not going anywhere."

Absolutely nothing inside me argued otherwise. Ethan, oddly, remained the constant here, while everything else—job, family, living situation—was in flux.

I'd assumed the worst, but he showed up anyway. And he called me his *girlfriend*. I could lean on Ethan. I trusted him. And yes...I loved him. I loved him so deeply, it frightened me. I had no idea how the next week would play out. Or the week after, or after that. I knew one thing. "I want you here."

Light sparked in his eye. "I admit, I was nervous to call you my girlfriend outright, but I went with it on a hunch."

I wanted him here, but dark thoughts clouded my head. "What are you doing here? I said you didn't have to come."

"Remember, caroling is mandatory?" He smiled faintly, not pushing too hard. "I wouldn't leave you to the wolves."

I lifted my chin. "You don't owe me anything." False confidence for the win.

"I don't fall back on my promises."

My throat tightened. "Aren't you mad at me?"

I'd spent the ten minutes in my closet, and then some, letting murky to pitch-black thoughts reign free in my mind. I couldn't see how Ethan and I could ever work. We had history, a loving, meaningful history, but I didn't belong here. I didn't belong with Ethan. Here, I'd forever be a Holly attached to my family's reputation, which had to be sullied by now. What was worse than sullied? Foully contaminated?

"Mad? At you?" Ethan moved closer. "Never. I signed on knowing the competition was ridiculous. Look, I don't know what's going to happen, but it's not over yet." He glanced past me for a beat before landing a kiss at my forehead. "Let's take this one day at a time."

My insides nearly combusted. I wanted so much to live in one single day, but my brain couldn't help advancing to our future. That image was murkier than ever. I simply could not envision it.

But Ethan came anyway, despite me pushing him away.

"All of this is meaningless if Grans is choosing who inherits," I said. "She is *forcing* us to carol."

"Think of this as the meta game. If we bounce now, it will count against us. Your brothers are here. Rafe and Riley are here. They're all here. If the competition was truly over, they'd be out at Everett's for the buffet."

"Who is Everett?"

"Everett's Dining—the restaurant on the east end of town? They do a big buffet the Saturday before Christmas."

I studied Ethan. This was the man I'd declared love to. He knew the town buffet schedule.

He smiled easily. "Their prime rib is no joke."

A red and green striped scarf wrapped around Ethan's neck and tucked into his hooded sweatshirt. Over top, the work coat he wore at the tree farm. "You're going to boil in all those layers."

"I'm prepared in case a lady catches a chill." He pulled me to him for a gentle kiss.

I lost myself in the moment, but the moment was momentary.

Grans entered the square flanked by her judges. In my head, a hard-hitting techno beat played as they approached in slow motion. Wool coats, plaid scarves, and gray hairs. This was a troupe with a menacing need to vocalize holiday merriment.

Cara eyed the judges, all present except TL. "I thought the competition ended."

"These are my *friends.*" Grans wore a glittery holly pin at her lapel that I wouldn't doubt hid a poison dart. "We're focused on the event tonight. Here are the song sheets." She handed out packets stapled together.

More prospective carolers gathered, given this was another Holly Days organized event. I couldn't help notice murmurs and stares our direction. Several clusters of people gave us a wide berth.

The coordinator sorted us into groups and passed out more song sheets. We were provided with a printed map of a designated section of town where we were expected to belt out holiday tunes.

My fury grew legs. "This is like a coordinated sonar attack." I waved the map at Ethan. "This, a battle plan. How can you not see how forceful this is?"

"I like Christmas caroling. I do this every year."

Since we were dating now, and he was my boyfriend, was this my future? Singing songs at people against their will?

Ethan nudged me with his elbow, obviously filing my reaction in the Over category. But as we marched with our group to a residential block couched within the downtown, a realization solidified.

This would be my life if I moved back. Ethan loved holidays. The whole holiday machine involved him and his Christmas tree farm. By default, being together, I would become part of the holiday machine.

The group began the first song from the packet. Each note stabbed my skin, each line grated at my nerves. *I hated this.*

Yes. I hated singing holiday songs on the street like we were bestowing some kind of gift. This was not like middle school chorus and our performance at the mall. The mall *invited* us. These people were just trying to eat their dinner and watch *Jeopardy!*

We walked the block, cut over to another street, and continued caroling. A husky baritone sporadically showed off vocal runs as if auditioning for *The Voice*. Little kids in the group skipped ahead and waved at the gullible suckers who flipped on their porch lights and gathered at front windows. The fiction collections supervisor from the library filmed it all with her phone. Great holiday content, if you were into that sort of thing.

Which I wasn't. I could barely stand pretending.

Right with them, Ethan sang along, never once questioning why I didn't join in.

I would never be the jolly Christmas fan he deserved. I honestly never wanted to go street caroling again in my life. The bake sale I didn't mind as much, but none of it was my jam. The Holly Games were meant to be a one-time event for me.

The storm cloud over my head hung thick all the way to town square after we cleared our route. Because the singing hadn't stopped. No, our group kept on singing. This was the pits, but I'd done it. Check it off the box.

Hot chocolate waited for us in the square. Too eager to taste it, the scorching liquid burned a patch on my tongue.

Bah Humbug indeed.

Ethan wandered off to chat with the librarian from our group, leaving me to sulk privately.

I caught recognizable names spoken from hushed voices on the other side of the bushes by the cocoa stand. Rafe's voice carried over.

"I don't want to be a disappointment to you and the kids," he was saying.

I angled myself into a spot where the bushes parted.

Brianne stood in front of him. "We just want you home *with* us. That's all we've ever wanted. I don't care where we live or what house we live in. Only that we're together."

"I know my travel schedule put a strain on you. I'm sorry. If I hadn't taken this promotion, I'd be out of a job same as Marlowe."

I shifted farther into the shadows. It shouldn't have been a comfort knowing Rafe's job was unstable. I'd taken my job cut so personally, even though everyone told me the layoff was a numbers game for the company. I was more than a number. So was Rafe, even if I still felt steamed at him at the moment. Job instability was hard no matter what, and he had a family to support.

"Won't you be upset if we don't inherit the house?" Rafe went on to Brianne. "It's our family legacy."

"The house is *huge*. And old. I don't know if I'm interested in the upkeep."

I couldn't hear Rafe's response, but I heard what his wife said back. "And you owe your cousin an apology. She looked very upset."

At the sound of footsteps, I pivoted from the bushes and walked straight into Grans. "Oh! So sorry, Grans." Thankfully, I'd drained my hot chocolate so nothing spilled on her pristine coat.

"How was caroling?" she asked.

Torture. "Fine. Good."

"Mmhm." She looked past me to where Rafe and Brianne had been talking, but I didn't dare turn to peek. "I'm disappointed I lost control. I should have stopped the personal snipes before they escalated."

I was glad she hadn't. "They said what they meant. Now instead of us dancing around who deserves the house, we know where we stand."

Grans glowered, but I wouldn't soften the blow. We were competitive by nature and apparently pretty judgmental about each other. Big surprise why I needed to establish my own identity apart from the family.

She rested a hand at my back. "You lost your job. Marlowe, I wish you'd told me. Are you okay financially? Do you need help with rent?"

I bristled. "I'm fine. I'll get another job."

"You cared about your work. You even received an employee recognition award. It's a shame your accomplishments didn't have more merit with your employer."

She remembered the award? I'd received it last year, when all I'd seen for my future were gleaming ladders pointed high.

Ethan lingered nearby, now talking with a guy we went to school with. Ethan deserved to get what he needed for the tree farm. If I had any chance left at the house, I needed to be honest with Grans. Give this one more shot for Ethan's sake.

"Actually, my roommate is moving out too." I filled her in about Anna's engagement. "With no job and an apartment lease ending, I'm not sure I have much to go back to."

"You've built a life there. Haven't you?"

Sure. Maybe? That temporary sense never quite left after grad school. Almost like I was biding my time until something else. I just couldn't figure out the something else. Only Anna had a window into my personal life.

One solid, close friend. That was the life I'd built in California. And she was ready to move on to her next adventure. Our phase of life was phasing out.

Grans' expression softened as much as she allowed for it. "You're young. You'll figure things out. I'm confident in that."

I swallowed. "The house...when you announced you wanted to pass it on, immediately I knew I wanted it. I can't imagine the house belonging to anyone else. Is that selfish? I'm not even sure what I'd do with it. I just know it's important. And the land, the family name, all of it is really, really important. More important than I realized until—" Right this moment? "Until I came home."

Grans made a *hmm* sound I wasn't sure how to interpret. She squeezed me in a one arm hug. "I'm glad you're here, Marlowe. It means a lot."

I desperately wanted to know how Grans would determine who inherited the house. But she simply smiled in her own guarded way. She steered me toward the rest of the family.

"Thank you all for coming out tonight," she said to Ashe and others in front of us. "We have a week until Christmas Eve. Hollybrooke House at two p.m. Dinner with gifts to follow."

And with that, she left.

Chapter 23

Ethan

I could tell Marlowe was going through a thing or two. She'd pushed me away earlier, instantly signaling she needed time to process. I decided to make it easy on her and left without putting up a fight. Besides, I'd done enough fighting.

Marlowe had always needed space to deal with things. Even as kids, when she didn't get her way or her brothers teased her, she'd fume for show, then retreat to lick her wounds. She always sprung back.

But that was then and this was now. We'd lived years apart from each other, forming new habits. As much as both of us had changed in small ways, I believed at our core, we were probably the same as we'd always been.

She despised caroling. So what? Public, cheerful singing wasn't for everyone. None of that mattered—whether she liked holiday stuff or not. I needed to show her how seriously I considered our relationship. I would support her no matter what.

The town square emptied out as her family dispersed and the shops closed for the night.

"You're coming with me," I told her.

She held up her car keys. "But I drove."

"Murdoch likes his alone time. You've been keeping him busy. Come on."

She followed, but with skepticism. "We're not going to more light shows, are we?"

"I promise, no torture."

I set the truck's heat to a healthy blast and set off. She flipped on the holiday station.

"You don't have to bother." I went for the stereo's digital keypad. "You've been through enough."

She stopped my hand with hers. "I...like this song." She cleared her throat. "It's okay."

I doubted she was serious, but maybe? "It's a good snow soundtrack." I liked this sort of snow. Light and fluffy before the heavier stuff came through and required a snowplow. And...it was romantic. I was a sucker for early snowfalls leading into Christmas. With my favorite girl at my side, this made for another moment I'd remember for a long time.

We didn't have to go far to reach the destination.

Marlowe perked up beside me. "Ethan, you can't be serious. You're taking us back to high school?"

I drove past the blocky structure to the surrounding sports fields. All the way to the farthest corner of the parking lot bordering the football field. Opposite the field, gentle hills dotted with scattered pines created a pleasant view.

"We used to hang out here." The realization unfolded as she spoke. "When Ashe played football and we got bored, us kids were allowed to run around out here as far as the tree line." She squinted through the dark. "And later, in high school, we'd lay in the grass over there."

She said *we,* though it was she and her friends without me most of the time. In front of us, the overhead lights cast a soft stage for the snow to swirl.

Marlowe sank into her coat. "It's still pretty, just like I remember."

"Yeah. I always liked how this area didn't get built up. I come out here to think. Sometimes, I come here and read."

"You do that now? You sit in a parked car at a high school and read a book?"

"Not during school hours. I'm not trying to be creepy. Call me nostalgic, but I get clarity when I come here."

"I didn't think you liked high school."

Her experience differed from mine. "I didn't love every second of it, but I didn't mind it." I craned my neck to look at our former school building. "See those windows there on the second floor? In American Lit, I'd stare out the windows to these trees. I wanted to be out here. Working with my hands."

"You always loved the outdoors."

"The tree farm made sense to me. It's not easy work, but it's always come easily for me. I've worked the tree lot in some way since I could walk. It's my life. I figured I could stay in Crystal Cove and, you know, keep the same life going. If I'm honest, I'll admit I always felt like a piece was missing."

"A Costco?" Marlowe grinned.

"Yeah, I base my life around bulk shopping." There she was, increasing space between us again. Almost like she knew where this conversation headed. "Marlowe, I've missed you. Even when I'm not trying to think of you, you're there in so many places. But I want you to know, I'm proud of you for leaving. You needed to. I hope you don't feel guilty for making your own life away from here. Or feel like you have to move back because of...because of us. Not that you would—"

"Ethan—"

"I'd never want you to feel resentful of small-town life." I rushed to get the words out. "I know Crystal Cove isn't where you always dreamed of living."

"I feel like I've been in a holding pattern since school ended. I could always count on another semester to guide my plans. And then the job, and moving up. Now that I was forced to stop and take a look around, I know I need to make a change."

Moving on could mean a hundred—a thousand, a million—different directions. Most of those directions probably did not include the small northwest corner of Illinois.

I unhooked my seatbelt and turned to Marlowe. "So much is in the air right now, but I want you to know, I'd give this all up for you. Wherever. Whenever."

Her mouth slightly parted. She shook her head. "No. Ethan, I would never ask you to do that."

"I know you wouldn't. That's why it's an offer. I want you to know I'm here for you. For us. I'm not holding anything back."

"The farm—it's your life. You need the farm. All of this—" she spun her hand in the air "—was to help you reach your dream."

I wasn't giving up just yet, but maybe giving up wasn't what I'd assumed. Maybe giving up meant not trying at all for the thing—the person—I wanted most.

She rubbed at her eye. "I still can't imagine..." She trailed off.

"What? What can't you imagine? Because I can imagine it. I imagine us. It's only the background that shifts."

Marlowe let out a breath before pulling me toward her. Our mouths crashed against each other. Intense kisses, unlike how we'd kissed before. How was it possible to have so many different kisses with one person? I could spend years, a lifetime, discovering new kisses with Marlowe.

It had always been her. Marlowe was the lost piece. She never belonged to me, but part of me went with her when she'd left. First figuratively, when she'd still been here but spent her time with new friends, then for real, when she'd gone away for college.

She'd needed to go, and I'd needed to let her. I'd fully expected I'd move on with my life.

Then she came back and all those good intentions meant nothing. These whirlwind past few weeks kept pointing to one person: her. It was like a light flicked on and all the required pieces for my life became visible. I simply needed to put them together. I wanted Marlowe in my life, and if I had to go where she went, then I'd go.

When we finally came up for air, she trailed a finger along my jawline. "There's so much I don't know."

"We can figure it out together." This felt exhilarating. We could chart new waters together—or whatever charting meant. "I just know I want to be with you."

She smiled. Hopeful, but worried. "My brain feels like this future feature montage, like a boy band supercut of endless possibilities. I can't pin down any one thing."

"One day at a time. That's how we look at this."

We kissed again, letting our futures and worries scatter to another day.

Chapter 24

Marlowe

The next day I woke to a text from Ashe. A group text including me, my siblings, cousins, and their spouses. Not Ethan and not Grans.

Ashe: *Let's meet and figure this thing out*

The responses threaded down to discuss times and locations.

I fired off a message. *Grans will be out for a day trip to Galena with her friends. The house is ours*

I winced at my wording and added a second text: *I mean the house is empty*

Shawn: *Hey I'm here too. What am I, chopped minced meat?*

Shawn: *That's a holiday delicacy in the UK for those of you who don't watch the bake off show*

Cara: *You mean a mince pie? I bet you've never tried one.*

Ashe: *LOL*

Shawn: *Have too!*

I rolled my eyes and flipped to another new message. This one from Ethan. My body instinctively warmed at the memory of last night in his truck. Talking, kissing, and thinking forward but only forward enough. He'd give up his world for me. That's what he'd told me. Dream words any person newly in love with their oldest and longest crush would be desperate to hear. *I'd give it all up for you.*

Ethan was more than a crush at this point. We weren't kids. We were adults with responsibilities and demands. And still, he'd give up what he had for me.

Ethan: *I'll be busy at the farm this week but I'm still in for the gingerbread contest.*

Me: *Gingerbread? In this economy?*

Me: *That was a joke. It's a no on the gingerbread. The competition is over, so we're off the hook. The…candy hook, I guess.*

No one else in the family planned on continuing with the gingerbread house competition. For invented points that no longer mattered? No, thank you. I could use the supplies I already bought to make a janky gingerbread with the kids. No judging required.

A full minute passed before Ethan responded.

Ethan: *Sure, if that's what you want. I thought it might be fun.*

Fun like caroling. Fun like a chaotic light show set to holiday music. I fell against my pillow. "Why do I hate *festivities*?" I questioned to my bedroom's four walls.

The walls stared back. They did not reply.

I tried to imagine a life where Ethan left to sing publicly at random people while I… What exactly would I do if I lived here? Crystal Cove didn't offer the jobs and salaries I could make in San Jose. Not like I'd looked for any open jobs here, or any remote work either. Regardless, I was doubtful. Maybe the mega pharmaceutical company nearby had openings. My qualifications likely fit something there.

But I couldn't see myself commuting from little Crystal Cove to the big business megaplex, taking what I did in my California life and inserting it here. The pieces didn't fit.

And Ethan. I loved him. I loved his kindness. His familiarity. How we had so much to catch up on, but none of it involved explaining myself. He knew me and he knew my heart.

My cold, dark, holiday-loathing heart.

He'd told me he loved me anyway. How love was unconditional. Could we make it work during the holidays? He'd go a-caroling while I did anything else but? I didn't hate baking, I just wasn't very good at it. And driving around looking at holiday lights so long as we never visited that showboating nightmare with the timed music ever again.

Could it work? Could *we* work? Ethan believed we could. Now I needed to believe it.

I heaved myself out of bed and headed for the shower.

My siblings and cousins were eager to *figure this thing out* and showed up at the house by eleven a.m. We convened in the library with kids either elsewhere at friends' houses or parked in the family room watching a movie.

Ashe stood in front of the built-in bookcases while the rest of us pulled in chairs from the dining hall. We settled in the room. Shawn positioned himself next to Ashe and stood to his full height.

"I have an idea," Ashe stated.

"As do I," said Shawn.

"Can you give it a rest and let me talk?" Ashe elbowed Shawn.

Shawn jerked out of his reach. "You're not the only one with ideas. I can stand here and share ideas too."

Cara left her chair. "Okay, here's what we're not doing." She pointed between the two brothers. "You two—take a seat. I vote the spouses and Riley lead this discussion since you men can't seem to stop bickering."

True as her words, the men bickered that they couldn't be trusted to lead the meeting.

"What about Marlowe?" Brianne asked.

Brianne, who I rarely spoke to because, well, she always seemed occupied by more important things, was the one to speak up for me. The person I spent the least time with in this extended family.

Cara blushed. "Sorry, Marlowe. I didn't mean to leave you out."

Just a natural inclination to forget me. Nothing new.

The disputing continued. Cara clapped loudly twice. "I have the floor!" She used her *Mom isn't joking* tone and the guys shut right up. Begrudgingly, Ashe and Shawn sat down.

"This isn't about men versus women," Cara continued. "We need to solve the issue with the house. Grans was right—this fighting between us must stop. She shouldn't have to decide who inherits the house. We should determine who gets the house among ourselves. A group consensus."

Oh sure, easy. We couldn't agree without arguing on who had the right to *stand by the bookcase,* let alone who should inherit a family treasure.

"Ashe and I talked last night," Cara said. "I showed him research I did on family trusts. One idea we had is to create a trust where all of the grandchildren have equal stake. Then, the house ownership is transferred to the trust. Not to any single person. All of us would own the house. Any decisions on the house and land would require consensus from all partners."

"So you're guaranteeing a lifetime of arguing," Riley added in a dry tone.

"We would need a common goal," Cara said. "Let's be brutally honest here. Show of hands: who actually wants to live in this house?"

Murmurs coursed through the room. No one immediately raised a hand. In fact, no one raised a hand at all.

"It's just..." Riley started. "The house means a lot to all of us. It's hard knowing Grans wants to move on. I assumed Reece would celebrate every Christmas and holiday here until she left for college—and beyond. Losing the house would be...difficult. But it's a lot of house to take on myself."

"The house is beautiful, but we have busy lives," Brianne said. "The upkeep would be incredibly time consuming. Grans hires a cleaner, and even then, there are rooms she closes off and doesn't use at all."

Rafe grumbled but didn't offer a counterpoint.

"It's important to keep the house *in the family*," Shawn said.

Ashe raised a brow. "You'd move here from Florida?"

He shrugged. "Maybe as summer house."

Cara scanned the group, assessing the reluctant responses. "If we take out the individual, and combine our interests, we have better options. The house doesn't need to be a burden."

As much as I loved the house and jumped on the chance to inherit, the past few weeks had shown me I wasn't certain it fit to live here and take on the responsibility. But if that was true, why had I been so insistent on winning?

Ethan. Who wasn't here. He hadn't been invited and honestly? I hadn't considered him in the context of this meeting until this moment. When Ashe said we needed to gather and figure this out, I saw this room of people. Not Ethan.

With the competition done, I couldn't leave him in the dust. He said he'd give up his life for me—wherever, whenever. I couldn't let him. His life and his dream was his tree farm. His family legacy meant the world to him.

No, I needed to fix this. I needed to give Ethan what he truly wanted and deserved.

I raised my hand. "Hypothetically speaking, if we all decide to do this group family trust thing, then I want to sell a small part of the land to Ethan Sawyer to expand the tree farm. Regardless of what happens to the house, that's what I want."

Rafe snorted. "We're not handing off land to your *boyfriend*."

Shawn wore a smug expression. "Well, well. Everyone assumed I'd be the first to parcel out the land for profit, but turns out Marlowe had her own agenda the whole time. You're in cahoots with the Sawyers!"

Chatter coursed through the room.

"The Sawyers have been neighbors for decades," Riley pointed out. "We don't use that land anyway and it would help a local business. I like the idea."

"*We* aren't using the land because *we* don't own it yet," Shawn said. "And you all hassled me for wanting to sell it off, so that's the last thing I'll vote for."

My stomach turned. This was not going well.

"We need to put to a vote if we're even doing this family trust," Rafe said, though with less combative energy than he'd had in previous weeks. "I'm for the trust, but not for dishing out land to whoever we like for the hour."

A direct hit. As if cycling through guys hourly had ever been my personality. I wasn't sure how that would even work apart from a reality dating show.

"Agree," Ashe said. "Discussion is closed on selling any part of the land until the trust is agreed upon and a done deal. All in favor, say aye?" He looked to each of us.

Every adult in the room raised a hand and agreed. Their eyes landed on me. Waiting.

I wouldn't give up on Ethan's dream, but right now, what choice did I have? My family finally reached consensus on what had divided us so sharply. The first big step of many.

I raised my hand. "Aye."

We spent the next two hours over snacks and coffee discussing potential plans. Cara deserved real credit. She maintained control over the group while pausing to prepare snacks for the kids in the house and designating Ashe to set up a craft to keep them busy.

Rafe called an attorney friend to get a referral to a firm specializing in estates and trusts.

Meanwhile, we brainstormed what to do with an aging Victorian house apparently none of us actually wanted to live in.

"Rental property," Shawn suggested. "Obvious."

"Who's going to rent this place?" Ashe asked. "The Monopoly guy?"

"The Monopoly guy lives in New York City," Adam chimed in from the doorway as he rolled a tiny toy car up the door frame. "On *Broadway.* Come on, Dad. *Duh.*"

"What if we leased the house to a bed and breakfast upstart—those have to exist right?" Riley asked. "Like the women in the books Grans reads, who return to their hometown after leaving for the big city and they set up shop at a B&B? And fall in love in the process."

Brianne gasped. "That's Marlowe." She turned to me. "You should run the house as a bed and breakfast. It would be incredibly charming."

"It'd make great ad copy," Shawn mused. "Prodigal, directionless daughter returns to small town. Your Hollybrooke story awaits."

Cara made a face. "That wasn't very good. How about this: a small-town romance come to life—stay at Hollybrooke suites: a sweet taste of...something. Okay, this is hard."

Riley jumped in with her own pitch.

"Hey—I'm *right* here," I said. "I don't want to run a bed and breakfast. I can barely cook. And the rest of running an inn involves what, washing sheets and towels?"

None of us seemed to know.

"The books and movies make it seem delightful." Brianne mindlessly tapped at the side of her coffee cup. "But it sounds like a lot of work."

They continued to chatter while my mind drifted. I was still miffed Shawn called me directionless, but the truth bit hard sometimes. I couldn't even imagine what my future here entailed for the time Ethan sang holiday carols. What would I be doing? What was my purpose here?

I raised my hand, even though this wasn't class and none of these fools were my teacher. "We talk so often about owning this land. When Cara questioned that ownership, it got me thinking. I think—no, I believe—we can do better. We can do something meaningful for our community with what we've been given."

Other than reconnecting with Ethan and my nieces and nephews, the most meaningful time I'd spent here was at the respite center. I wasn't qualified to work there, but if I moved back, I'd at least be able to sign on to the time commitment required to volunteer.

The tiny respite center making do in the corner of an administration building.

"Yeah, and?" Shawn sounded more curious than demanding.

A plan began to form. "I don't know if it will work, but I have an idea."

I texted Ethan. *Need to talk. When are you available?*

After checking for replies for ten minutes, I let him know we were at the house discussing what to do next. I left it vague, given all the details yet to work out, and set the phone aside. He'd told me this week would be busy. Right now, all the decision makers were here and available and we had a lot to figure out.

A real sense of excitement caught wind among my siblings and cousins. Assuming the trust idea worked out legally and all that, we could potentially lease, sell, or even donate Hollybrooke House to the county for use as a respite facility. Through my research, I'd read how respite facilities varied widely. Some offered houses or small complexes for overnight visits serving children in foster care or families with special needs children. They weren't limited to a playroom and a couple offices in a crowded administration building. Having a home-like setting with plenty of rooms to use for different needs could work well.

Once Shawn got going about real estate tax breaks, he and Rafe's interests appeared to align. Suddenly, they were budding philan-thropists, coming up with ideas to benefit the community with the Holly name front and center.

"Executer of the Holly Trust," Shawn announced. "I like that title. It suits me."

Ashe shook his head. "You'd be a trustee. One of many trustees with equal power to manage the assets."

"I like Executer better," Shawn grumbled.

"At least this idea might shine up the tarnished family reputation," Cara said. "The local My Hood forum is steamed up about the calami-ty in town square. They're speculating we've driven up the city's crime rate."

Ashe sat back in a squeaky leather chair. "Maybe we can get out of community service duty if we donate the house."

Cara cast him a lethal glare. "You need to serve your time. You know what you did."

Riley yawned and stretched. "Now the big question: do we wait for Christmas dinner to tell Grans, or tell her as soon as she gets back?"

We chattered among ourselves, feeling pretty proud of the progress we'd made.

Ashe stood. "We should look at the property lines and get a lay of the land while we're putting this plan together. Shawn, do you know where Grans stores the deed?"

Shawn crossed the room. "Isn't there a safe in this lower bookcase cabinet?" He knelt and opened the doors. "Bingo."

Ashe rubbed his hands together. "Nice. I'm pretty sure the combination is Gramps' and Grans' anniversary date." He lowered to the level of the safe.

Cara nudged him with her knee. "Well go ahead—put in the combination."

He angled to look at her. "It's uh…"

She rattled off the date from memory.

Ashe coughed. "Thanks. You know I'm not great at remembering dates." He tapped in the numbers and the safe beeped. The door unlocked.

"This is the least suspenseful escape room I've ever been in," Shawn quipped.

Ashe pulled out several large manila envelopes. Each wore labels from a label maker, making it easy to find the land deed and accompanying property map.

He spread the map across the large heavy desk in the room, now used more for decoration than business. We all hovered over it.

"Huh, what's this?" Ashe held up what looked like a sticky note that over time had lost its stick. "'Three acres to Stan Sawyer.' It's got Gramps' signature."

"Gramps planned to sell land to the Sawyers?" I leaned in to read the note. "Is there a date? Did he pass away before the deal?"

Rafe tapped the map. "Check this out. There's a faint line running here. Looks like it's marked in pencil. It parallels the farm border, but it's farther in toward the house."

Ashe blinked. "That looks like the farm's property line now. See how this ridge goes this direction? Here's the hill and their fence line. Me and the kids ran around out there the other day. This pencil line to the border—that gap might be three acres."

A growing sense of dread crept in. "What does this mean?"

Ashe emptied the folder. Only one other sheet remained and it had nothing to do with a land sale to the Sawyers. "It seems like Gramps gave this chunk of land to the Sawyers, but I'm not sure they actually own it. Which means part of their farm is built on Holly land."

Just then a figure shadowed the doorway of the library. Work coat and a plaid scarf. All eyes turned to Ethan Sawyer.

Chapter 25

Ethan

"Uh, hey everybody. What's going on?"

Marlowe, her siblings, and cousins—everyone but Emmaline—crowded around the library's big desk with what looked like a map spread across it. They all stared at me.

Ashe held up a small note. "Did you know about a land sale between your father and Gramps? Would have been at least seven years back. Maybe longer. There's no date."

My heart stilled. Was this what Marlowe wanted me here for? No, she'd texted at least an hour ago. Based on their expressions, this appeared to be a new discovery.

I tugged my scarf free from my neck. "Uh, I...yeah. It's a few acres."

"There doesn't seem to be paperwork for it," Ashe went on. "Does your dad have it?"

I shot a glance to Marlowe. I couldn't read her. She appeared confused, which made sense. A little hopeful, a dash something else.

I wasn't trying to hide anything. Might as well come out with it. "There's no contract. Dad said as much. It sounds like it was more of a neighborly agreement."

Riley looked between us. "Wait, so this is a different land deal than what you wanted Marlowe to give you?"

She'd asked them about giving me land? I scratched the back of my neck. "Yeah. That was a...different conversation." It was hard to know what to say with so many questioning eyes boring into my flesh.

"More land than what you already have on Holly property?" Rafe clarified.

Marlowe stepped away from the desk, seeming to retract into herself. "You knew? About this?" She pointed to the map.

This looked bad. Really bad. "Only recently. Very recently. It's...complicated."

"This is exactly why I said no land to boyfriends," Rafe muttered. "Look—his family already has several acres and they want more. For free."

"I never said free—" But my words were cut off by escalating voices. All but Marlowe, who stood silent.

"Now we know why this scrub was hanging around so much." Shawn approached, sizing me up as if we hadn't known each other for two decades. "Mooching off my baby sister to take our land."

The way he growled you'd think the guy was starring in a Western flick. "That's not true. It was never about that."

It being us, and the care and love I'd had for Marlowe practically my whole life, and *that* being the land deal. Which had been part of our partnership, but obviously not the only reason I'd been spending time with her.

"Do you even care about Marlowe?" Brianne threw up her hands. "Is the small-town B&B romance a total farce?"

Cara whistled sharply for our attention. "Okay, folks. We're not devolving into chaos for the umpteenth time. Ethan? Here's the deal. We've decided a few things about the house. No one person will inherit. We're proceeding with a family trust and looking into a few charity options. To come to this decision, we all agreed any discussion of selling land is off the table until we can determine the details of the trust."

I looked at Marlowe. She'd agreed not to discuss selling the land? Just like that, in a meeting I hadn't been invited to?

Right, because I wasn't a Holly. A fact I'd lost sight of the past few weeks. Of course I didn't get a vote. Wasn't this exactly what my brother warned me about? Trusting Marlowe to come through on the deal was a risk. In this case, it wasn't that she didn't want to fulfill her end, but she didn't have the power.

She'd been overruled. I should have known it would come to this. The Hollys did what they wanted, all the time, by their own rules. I might have been an honorary Holly accepted at Thanksgiving dinner, but when it came to property rights, I had no say.

I loved this family like my own, but this wasn't debatable. Unless you were a Holly, and then every aspect was up for debate.

What else could I do but agree? They'd already decided what was what. "Marlowe, I'm sorry about this extra land thing complicating our deal—"

"There's no deal," Shawn seethed. "Because none of that land is *yours.*"

Ashe shouldered in front of Shawn and nudged him aside. "Alright, cool off. I doubt the Sawyers conspired against us. Let's talk this through."

Marlowe skirted the edges of the room until she reached the door. She opened the second of the French doors to move past me. "You said you weren't holding anything back," she stated in a low voice meant for me only. "I believed you."

"I never meant to lie. Telling you would have complicated this more than it needed."

She left the room but glanced behind her as she headed down the hall. I followed.

We landed in the kitchen. She paced the length of the room with one hand hovering as if ready to gesture. "Why didn't you trust me? That's the issue here. I want to help you. If I'd known just how much you needed the land—all of it—I might have approached this in a completely different way."

"Trust? You say you want to help me but you let your family steamroll over you. They were always going to have the upper hand and you know it."

She stopped pacing and fired a fierce look at me. "Are you saying I gave up on you? We needed to come to an agreement over this house before we could even consider discussing the land. Believe me, I tried. Only then we find out there's more to the story. That *you* knew about."

My frustration let loose. "We should admit this idea was never going to work. I was the dumb one to believe it might."

We fell silent with only voices carrying over from down the hall.

I was mad at myself for believing I could get what I wanted, but also how I'd put Marlowe in the position to fight her family. She'd spent years staying away for this specific reason, to establish herself on her own, and I'd dunked her right back in. Of course her family would keep seeing her as the baby to protect. A child, not an adult with equal share on family matters. That's how it had always been.

Families rarely changed. It was naive for either of us to believe ours might.

My anger wasn't at Marlowe. Not at all. "Hey. I'm sorry. I didn't want to make this all more stressful by telling you we didn't own those acres. I just learned about it myself. It puts the farm in more of a bind if we owe money for what we're already using, plus asking for more—if that's even possible now. Anyway, it's not your job to fix my family's business. I shouldn't have ever made the deal with you. That's on me, not you."

But then we wouldn't have had this time together. I didn't regret these past few weeks. Or what I'd told her last night. "Look, I meant it when I said I'd give this up. Maybe this is a big old sign telling me the farm isn't going to work out. It'd be better if my folks sold the property and rode off into the sunset on their cruise ship of choice. I'll figure out something else to do with my life."

Marlowe's shoulders slumped. "But you love your farm. You don't want to do something else. If you did, you'd be doing that."

"Just because I want the farm to succeed doesn't mean it will. It might be time to call it quits. I'm not a failure because the farm didn't work."

Her back went rigid.

I wanted to yank the words from the air. "Hey, I didn't mean—"

"No, I got your meaning. A career setback isn't a life altering crisis for you. Got it."

Her prickly tone told me I'd hurt her as I'd feared. "That's not what I meant. I'm sorry. And you're right. I want the farm to work out. It's the thing I'm good at and I want to grow the business. But I also love you and want you in my life. I don't know if I get to have both."

Right now, I might not get either. And maybe neither was for me to *have* in the first place.

"You don't deserve this mess." She pointed at herself. "Once we get this trust thing underway, I'll do everything I can to sort out the land issue so it's fair for you and your family. I don't want anything else getting in the way."

I moved toward her. "If you're implying you are in the way, you aren't."

"Ethan. You have a stable job with room for growth. All I've done is muck it up."

I liked how she said *muck it up,* but nothing else about this conversation was worth liking.

Marlowe leaned against the counter by the sink. "Grans is going to have a fit when she hears about all this."

A startled laugh fell out of me. "You haven't told your grandmother about these plans? She's the one who's supposed to determine the inheritance. And here you thought I was leaving out details."

Her cheeks colored. "She's been out all day."

"Which is perfect timing for a family meeting to exclude her."

She couldn't hide her guilt. "Think she knows about the farm land?"

"Honestly, I have no idea." One thing about this family that never shocked me—they were always full of surprises.

Marlowe and I parted on shaky terms. Not earthquake shaken, but maybe lightly shaken, not stirred? Man, I really wanted to watch the latest 007 movie with her. It made our combined Movies to Watch list.

Who was I kidding? Movies were a distraction to the real issue. Marlowe was loyal to her family first and foremost. As we'd established, I was not a Holly. I didn't want to be a Holly when it came to Marlowe, but it also meant I definitely didn't factor into deciding anything to do with the house, the land, or their family.

I'd told Marlowe I was taking off and we could talk later. I for sure didn't want to stick around for when their grandmother returned. By the time I made it out to my truck, she'd already texted.

Marlowe: *Let's give this some time*

I sat in the truck for a beat, looking at the house. She only had another week here, through Christmas. So this was what, time for her to pack up and head out?

I drove to the farm. The last few days were a lot to take in. Getting away from the Holly family in general seemed like the right move.

Shoppers swarmed the farm, still surprising me how many people waited until the week leading into Christmas to buy a Christmas tree. Business was good, except we were running out of trees to sell. Not the best situation for a tree farm.

After sprucing up the decimated sales area where the porch pots and door wreaths had been—now branch scraps and errant pine needles—I headed to the trailer office.

"Hey, look who's here." Dad was all smiles.

"What's got you in such a good mood?" My boot hit the side of a wooden Santa parked on the floor by the door. The Santa tipped over and I left it. That was my mood.

Dad nodded toward the open chair, but I preferred to stand. He shrugged. "Talked to Leon Sanderson and his daughter Kylie. They're thinking of getting out of the cherry business."

The Sandersons owned a cherry tree farm not far from us. The local farmers all knew each other and talked shop over coffee regularly. More of a Dad thing than my scene. I eventually heard all the coffee chatter from him anyway.

I grunted a response which signaled Dad to keep talking. "Told him about your plans to expand the tree farm and they got a real interested look."

"Huh. Why's that?"

"Cherry farming isn't as lucrative as it once was. Leon will talk your ear off on why. Kylie's real keen on it being time to evolve. I told her,

'You sound like my son.' Anyway, they might be up for chatting with you about these *evolving ideas*." Dad grinned.

I found myself taking a seat anyway. And tipped the wooden Santa back upright. "I don't know if I have it in me to do what this farm needs. The Hollys know about the borrowed land—on a sticky note? Really?—and I'm not sure they're into the idea of selling more land, having not known about the acres we already have."

Dad let out a long sigh. "I always planned to talk to Emmaline formerly. Pretty sure she knows and doesn't mind."

"Pretty sure doesn't mean much when the house is changing ownership and they need an accurate property map."

"You don't say?"

I filled him in on the latest. I skipped a lot of details, mainly about me and Marlowe declaring love for each other and anything else related to our relationship. And my own thoughts on whether we could even call what we had a relationship. It hurt too much to think about her, but also? TMI for a convo with my dad.

"Anything else you care to mention?" he asked.

Definitely not any of the Marlowe stuff. "What else is there?"

He tapped at his phone and faced it toward me. "This you and one of the Holly boys wrestling in town square?"

My eyes fell shut. "Yeah. That happened."

He chuckled. "Next video I see of you better be picking up road trash right along with the Holly clan."

How he knew about the community service, I had no idea.

"I've got eyes and ears everywhere, son. A legendary dust-up like that? Word spreads like wildfire."

Town gossip for the win. "Sorry, I lost my head. I'll do what's necessary to make up for it."

"I believe you. How's Marlowe?"

"She's fine."

He gave me a steady, stern look. His features softened. "I know you've had feelings for her a long while."

Nope. I stood, ready to bolt.

"Your mother and I had a rocky start too. Did you know I asked her out three years before she said yes?"

I nodded. I'd heard the story. They met early in college but didn't start dating until the end. When they discovered they were the only two sober people at a party their friends dragged them to, they dropped off their friends at home and went on to a 24/7 diner where they talked until sunrise. They were inseparable ever since.

"Sometimes people need to work out their own kinks before they see what's right in front of them," he said.

"We both need time to clear our heads," I admitted. "So whatever the farm needs this week, I'm all in. No distractions."

I could tell he wanted to say more. Dad wasn't a chatty guy, but he could get going if he thought he had a point. "Talk to the Sandersons and see if you like their idea. Don't let this one go. I have a good feeling."

He handed me a phone number on paper torn from a scratch pad. I plugged the number into my phone's contact list, then pitched the paper into recycling. I headed for the door.

"And, son?"

"Yeah?"

"I have a good feeling about the girl, too. Keep your head up and don't do anything stupid."

Chapter 26

Marlowe

One week remained until Christmas. My goal? Stay as busy as possible. Busy kept my mind off of Ethan. And I had a lot to do.

Rafe managed to schedule a video call with an estate attorney. All of us gathered at his house—away from Grans' curious ears—to learn the role of trustees and our options for managing the house.

Brianne and her killer networking landed us another meeting about charitable foundations. If we sold off portions of the land, the money could be used to start a foundation offering community grants, managed by our family. Even more exciting possibilities.

Beyond that, my to do list included gift shopping and assisting Grans with sorting through the attic and the spare bedrooms. Any furniture she wouldn't have room for at her new place, she planned to offer first to the family. Then, she'd work with antiques dealers and resale shops, and eventually donate the rest.

Every day I wanted to see Ethan. I wanted to run to him and tell him we'd figure this out. But I needed to sort my own life before I even considered adding him in. I needed my own plans. My own agenda.

Over Christmas Double Eve dinner (that would be two days before Christmas), we told Grans about our plan for the family trust. We were too excited and far along in our plans to wait any longer. Grans merely smiled as we laid out our ideas.

After eating and sending off the kids to play games, we brought out the land deed and map and the now infamous formerly sticky note. Ashe took the lead. "Did you know about this?"

Grans examined the note and shook her head. "He never was much of a land baron, my Alan. Well, that's a kink in your plans. What are you going to do about it?" She looked at us.

Shrugs and silence all around. I pressed my tongue against a sharp tooth, willing myself not to jump in. Ethan's words floated back. *You let your family steamroll over you.* I couldn't stand having my suggestion squashed, but we all agreed not to discuss selling land until the trust was fully established.

Then again, steamrolling—ouch, right? Speaking up when it mattered could be the way to get them to take me seriously. I never had trouble speaking up in school or at work when I had an opinion to offer. Only with my family.

Because I was the baby and they never listened. Well, this baby was all grown up.

Cara poked Ashe in the arm. "Well?"

Ashe let out his breath in a huff. "It's not up to me. We'll all be trustees, so we'll put it to a vote?"

Grans delicately folded her hands in front of her. "You'll need a vote to determine the right thing to do?"

Trick question! Panicked looks streaked across the table. For once, Shawn kept his mouth shut. Rafe and Brianne exchanged glances while Ashe and Cara elbowed each other. Riley shot a look to her parents, but Uncle Joe and Aunt Sunny existed in their own world, having created a healthy distance over the inheritance.

Here was my chance. "We should meet with the Sawyers and discuss what they'd like to do. We shouldn't assume anything. At the very least, we should formalize the land deal Gramps made. Perhaps it's not currently legal, but we could ensure we aren't harming the Sawyer business. Like we discussed, we can do better. We can think less about how this house benefits us and instead how we can use what we have to benefit others. That's honoring our family legacy just as much as one of us holding onto the property. Maybe even more so."

Shawn opened his mouth and I held up my finger. A thrill of satisfaction hit when Shawn let me continue without interruption. "And before anyone comments about my relationship with Ethan, this is coming from me, not him. As a Holly, we honor our commitments. Gramps committed the land to the Sawyers and I believe he had the best intent. This would be to honor Gramps as much as the Sawyers."

The silence grew less awkward. Did I sense an air of respect?

"That's entirely reasonable," Ashe said.

Yes. Ashe was tough to impress, and I still appreciated approval from my oldest brother. Old habits held strong.

"We'll need to officially vote once the trust is established," Rafe pointed out. "But I'm open to a sit-down with the Sawyers to clear any misunderstandings."

Brianne sighed loudly. "Oh, let's give them the land and call it a day." She directed her attention to me. "For *love*."

This time laughter filled the silence. My cheeks lit with heat. "Stop talking about my love life!"

Ashe laughed. "No way, it's cheap entertainment."

"Are we sure this Sawyer kid isn't using you, Marlowe?" Shawn cracked his knuckles. "I meant it when I said I'd protect my baby sister." He held up a hand. "I'd like to correct myself. My full, adult sister."

I gaped at him.

Shawn glanced to Cara who nodded. So subtle I could have missed it. Well, well. Maybe my family noticed more than I thought.

Grans continued to look generally pleased. "Despite a few bumps in the road, you all are a clever bunch who understand compassion. I trust you'll make good decisions together. If I believed any of you were truly cutthroat, I wouldn't have left the estate planning to you."

"But you didn't," I reminded her. "You told us you would decide and we went behind your back and planned this anyway."

Shawn kicked me under the table. "You're making it worse."

Grans smiled again. "Didn't I? Somehow, things went exactly as planned. Minus disgracing the town square's religious display."

Even if the town forgot, Grans wouldn't.

Grans played us. She knew we wouldn't tolerate having the decision made for us, which put us in the hot seat to figure out a plan on our own. Smart one, that Grans.

I had the feeling our trustees would make the right call on what to do with the tree farm land.

But that still left me with dozens of unanswered questions. Like, where would I live? Where would I work? Would I continue to push Ethan away, even though the last thing I wanted was more distance from him?

Since I hadn't helped a lick with cooking dinner, I took on dish duty. Grans followed me to the kitchen.

"I hope you'll invite Ethan to the house for Christmas if he can take time from his own family."

I edged the faucet to scalding. The sting of hot water dulled the hurt over Ethan. "I don't know."

"What was that mumble-jumble?"

Grans had great distaste for mumbled responses. Even worse when the response was: I don't know.

I shut off the water and spoke more clearly. "I'm not sure he'll want to. We left things kind of...unfinished."

"Well, unfinished sounds like you need to talk it out. Over holiday ham and pies."

"Not everything can be solved with pie, Grans."

She feigned a shocked posture. "Have you tried my blueberry crumble?"

"I'm serious. I don't have my life together. Ethan said he'd drop everything for me—*for me*—and I can't let him. I still need to go back to California. Pack up my things and then what? Do I stick it out there and find another roommate? Another job? My car is there. If I come back here, do I sell it? What about Murdoch? I've never sold a car before. I've only ever bought the one. I've never had to do any of this!"

My haphazard thoughts blurred and the unsettled feeling now morphed into a larger panic. Gentle arms encircled me.

"Being a young woman in her twenties is the hardest time I can think of," she said. "There's so much to decide. So much pressure. Your pressures are different from what I faced but no less difficult. You have so many choices. More than I had. I imagine that can be intimidating. What if you choose wrong?"

I looked at Grans. "That's exactly what I'm afraid of. What if I already chose wrong?"

"You've made thoughtful decisions so far. I was wondering if the idea of choosing wrong had you knotted up. My mind works the same way." She looked at me with all her years of experience and wisdom. "You're accomplished and independent. I couldn't ask for anything more. Your parents would be so proud."

My parents, more of a legend than a memory for me. I took Grans' word. If she was proud of me, I could believe my parents would be too.

I'd wanted so badly to prove I could stand on my own. I'd accomplished so much since leaving home. I'd graduated from college and graduate school, found a job in my industry, lived on my own, and created an identity apart from my family. I just convinced everyone to honor Gramps' land arrangement with the Sawyers. I *had* proven myself.

Now I needed to believe it. And believing I could stand on my own meant I could do that anywhere. Even here in Crystal Cove. I wasn't a failure if I came back. I also didn't need to stay here forever.

Grans nailed it. I had options. Exciting options. I could do *anything*.

"I don't know if I'll stay in Crystal Cove for good." Slowly, a plan emerged in my mind. "There are a lot of places to explore. But I'd like to come back and figure out my next move."

"I won't be moving for some time yet, so you have a room here. My condo will have a guest room. *One* guest room."

I faced Grans and gave her a hug. A real big one with a tight squeeze.

When I pulled away, tears streaked my face. "I love you. And I love this family. And I love one other person a whole lot and I don't know what to do about it."

She wiped my cheek with her finger. "I know, dear."

"You do?"

"Hard to get much past me. That man is head over heels for you. Do you have a Christmas gift for him?"

I was crying in the kitchen and she was asking about gifts? I sniffled. "You think I should?"

She patted my shoulder before drifting to the door. "I imagine he has one for you. Invite him for dinner and we'll see."

Chapter 27

Ethan

On Christmas Day, I knocked on the front door of Hollybrooke House carrying a covered glass dish packed with cheesy potato casserole. Over my shoulder, a backpack filled with presents. Santa in the Midwest minus the red coat and hat.

Ashe's youngest answered the door, this time as a human, not as a dog on all fours. "Oh. It's you." He turned. "MARLOWE! IT'S YOUR BOYFRIEND AND HE HAS A CASSEROLE!"

The doorway cleared of children and I stepped inside.

The smells hit me: cranberries at a low simmer on the stove, a drifting waft of honey ham, and a welcome hint of pine.

Marlowe appeared in a Christmas sweater. Thick green knit with a fabric gingerbread figure stuck to the front. The belly of the gingerbread functioned as a pocket with real, actual candy canes poking out.

I pointed, speechless.

"Hey. Come on in." She took the glass dish from me and headed down the hall.

"Are you going to explain the sweater?"

We reached the dining hall. "It was my gift from Ashe's kids. Mallory and Adam told me they picked out the best one because it's interactive. Here."

She set the dish down and handed me a candy cane. *From her sweater.*

"You must be counting the days until January."

She grinned. "Actually, I am, but for a different reason."

We had so much to say that had nothing to do with interactive holiday clothing. We hadn't exactly been on no speaking terms, but our texts the past week had been simple. Short and to the point.

I hated every second of not talking to her. While I needed space from the Holly family, I didn't want space from Marlowe. Just the opposite. But pressuring Marlowe into a relationship would be the quickest way to send her back to the West coast. I meant it when I said I'd follow her anywhere, but would she want me to? Yeah, she said she loved me, but she had a life in California.

Our lives had intersected again, but for how long?

I needed to handle this the right way. One day at a time. So I invited her to Christmas dinner with my folks. And she accepted. We were going there after this.

She'd invited me here immediately after I'd asked, and naturally I'd agreed. I could grumble how the Hollys always came first, but her family would forever have a larger-than-life sense about them.

"It's been a whole week," Marlowe stated.

Seven miserable days. Seven days without Marlowe. Seven days of diving into farm work and anything else to take my mind off her.

I spent a chunk of that time making her gift. No gift would be good enough, but this at least came from my heart.

"I brought presents." I swung the backpack off my shoulder. "Some are for the kids. One for your grandmother." I stumbled through my words. None of this was what I wanted to be talking about.

She took my hand, reading my awkwardness like a cry for help. "I have something for you too. Let's find somewhere—" a child shrieked in another room "—more private."

We ended up in her grandmother's office at the back of the house off the hall from the kitchen. Besides a desk and bookshelves, the room offered a bench seat by a window, and even better, a door that fully closed.

Without speaking, we embraced. Her hands traveled up my plaid flannel shirt and connected at the back of my neck. "Merry Christmas, Ethan Sawyer." Her voice came low and downright sexy.

"Bah Humbug, Marlowe Holly."

She tipped her head back laughing. "A humbug wouldn't wear this, right?" She looked down at the sweater.

"A humbug with a heart might."

"Tyler gave me this as a counterpoint." She hooked a finger beneath the sweater collar to reveal a necklace with a black sort of crystal pendant. "It's coal. Fake, but it's supposed to look like a lump of black coal. Maybe humbuggery runs in the family."

"Maybe so." I wanted to kiss her. So badly. We hovered in this in between zone of flirting and questionable futures. She looked so beautiful in her ridiculous sweater. Her beauty had nothing to do with her clothes or makeup. Joy radiated from her that couldn't come from those things.

Before I kissed her, before I let myself fall all over again, I had to know what was making her glow. "What's going on with you? You seem...happy."

She pressed her lips together and a big smile exploded she couldn't hold back. She returned both hands around my neck. "In January, I'm headed to California."

She let her statement sit a torturous beat before continuing. "To pack. I'm moving back. For now. To this house, first. To an apartment TBD."

Marlowe was coming back. She was coming home. "I—"

She pressed a finger to my mouth. Was I nuts to call this sexy too? Silencing me with a simple touch?

"I'm moving for me. To find what I want to do. I have a few ideas, but nothing set in stone." Her face grew more serious. "I wanted to make the decision myself before you and I saw each other again. Even if things don't work out between—well, I mean I want us to work out, but in case they don't, I wanted to decide on a plan regardless." She sighed with force. "I'm sorry for the dramatics with my family. I understand if I'm too much." She released her hands. "I'm not sure why I'm clinging to you—I'm sending a mixed message. Gosh, I am messing this up."

Marlowe was moving home and wanted us to work out. I'd heard all I needed.

I closed the distance between us and kissed her. She melted at my touch, slumping even, until she angled an arm around my neck and pressed in.

Another new kiss. How were they all so different? I tasted her joy, her minty excitement. Probably the candy canes, but all of it together tasted perfect and so very Marlowe.

We broke free. "I love you, Marlowe."

She responded with another kiss. Then: "I love you too, Ethan."

Our lips met again. Nothing, not pounding feet outside the door or a ringing kitchen timer could take me out of this room right now.

Eventually, Marlowe pulled back. "You said you had a present?"

"There's the holiday spirit." I took her wrapped gift from my bag.

We sat on the floor facing each other. She tore into the wrap. "Ethan, wow. You made this?"

"You liked the stamp, so... It's a welcome home key shelf. For wherever you end up hanging your house keys."

Her eyes watered. "It's perfect. Thank you." She tangled her fingers with mine. "I can leave it here since I won't need it for my trip to California." She paused. "A trip to California. Not going home to California. It already no longer feels like home."

I squeezed her hand. "Selfishly, I'm glad you feel that way."

"Selfishly, I am too."

"Why selfish for you? I'm the one who benefits."

"I resisted coming back for so long because it felt like the easy choice. It was almost like I sought out difficult circumstances." She shook her head. "Suddenly, the choice did feel easy. It's easy because I miss my family. I miss you. I don't need to be hung up on the past because the past is gone. If anything, nosy people in town are going to remember the Holly and Sawyer boys fighting in town square over anything I ever did."

"Can't argue there." I wished I could. "Speaking of town and reputations, I talked with some farm owner friends about a potential idea for our farms."

"Yeah?"

"They grow cherry trees, but the price they can sell cherries is the lowest it's been in decades. Overseas imports are taking the bulk of business at a fraction of the cost. They're interested in growing a new crop. Could be, they might want to grow Christmas trees."

She scooched closer. "What does that mean?"

"We're in early talks, nothing decided. But we could merge. Their land offers the space we need to grow more trees. Their experience farming means my folks can retire and leave the farm in good hands.

Rob could move on too—he's been restless. I'd have support. And more time and focus for the gift shop barn."

"I can't believe you're excited about a gift shop." Her grin gave her away.

"You think it's sweet."

"I love that you have a vision. A clear one." She kissed me on the cheek. "I'm proud of you for making your own way."

"Look at us. Adults getting things done." I had so many questions. "What will you do about work?"

"Grans suggested I take time to figure out the right fit. While I look for jobs, she provided the *generous* volunteer opportunity of helping her sort through the house. I've already made four spreadsheets for tracking donations and items marked for antiques dealers. We're considering leaving the dining hall table and chairs and some bed frames for the respite facility, if that all ends up working out. Then I have tracking spreadsheets for job hunting."

"Sounds like you'll be busy."

"It'll pass the time. No one's hiring right now anyway. Brianne is well connected and my family knows everybody else. I'm sure something will shake out."

"In Crystal Cove? Or beyond?" Only so much job opportunity existed in the area and surrounding small towns.

"Remote positions are options. Maybe a forty-minute commute to Rockford." She shrugged. "Weirdly, I'm not worried about it. It's like I have this sense of peace about my future now that I'm not fighting so hard about being seen as a successful, independent woman. I can just *be* a successful, independent woman."

She practically glowed. A beautiful, confident glow.

"Oh—speaking of nostalgia and other sentimental things, come on." She hopped up and stretched her hand out. "I have a present for you. Follow me."

I took her hand and stood. I swept her in another kiss. Her cascade of giggles sounded like music to my heart. Music to rival the holiday station.

We left the office for the family room, stepping over toy train tracks and a row of stuffed animal bystanders. Marlowe hefted a wrapped box from beneath the tree and handed it to me. "For you."

The box had some weight to it. I sat in a nearby chair and tore into the wrapping. Opening it revealed a sturdy leather utility apron. On the front pocket, a clip held a patch reading: Sawyer Woodworking Inc.

"For your potential second career." Marlowe tucked her hair behind her ear. "I had the patch made separately as a rush order. You don't have to use it."

"Not use it?" I stood and swung the top loop of the apron over my head. "I'm wearing this to dinner including the patch. I mean, look at all these pockets!"

She smiled a shy smile that nearly struck me speechless. She looked so beautiful right now. Yes, in the sweater. I would have been happy just seeing her on Christmas, but this gift? This was special.

And useful. "How did you know I needed a new work apron?"

"I noticed a pretty threadbare apron in the barn. More like *threads nowhere.*" She snort-laughed.

Yup, still beautiful.

She sprung toward the tree. "Okay, I have another gift for you because I wasn't sure on the apron."

She handed me a book with a ribbon tied around it. I tugged the ribbon free. A photo book. Inside, the pages began with a single photo of us as young kids. Probably three or four years old. We were at the farm posed by a tractor.

How it started, the page read in frilly cursive.

The next pages progressed through the years, from kids to teenagers, to high school graduation. We'd found time to take a photo together in our commencement robes.

Blank pages followed.

"Those are for the rest of the story," she spoke over my shoulder. "The *How it's going* phase of...us."

My throat tightened. "And you call yourself a humbug."

I hooked her close and kissed her. Beneath the glow of the Christmas tree lights, it was downright festive. Romantically festive.

"Back together?" Shawn asked from the doorway. He pointed at his eyes and then to me. "I'm watching you, Sawyer. You be good to my successful, adult sister." He moved on to the kitchen.

I looked at Marlowe. "That was interesting."

"He's working on it. Kind of like how I'm working on...everything." She laughed.

"Prepare for dinner," Cara called out from the kitchen. "That means hands should be washed!"

I spun Marlowe toward me. The coming weeks would be filled with change. With texts and coast-to-Midwest phone calls.

Those blank pages called to me. So many pages to fill.

Footsteps and voices sounded around us as the family moved to the dining hall for the big holiday dinner. Still, we stood in our little space by the tree, holding fast to this moment.

"I can't imagine anyone else I'd rather spend Christmas with," she said. "You, a rowdy family, and a child who no longer barks like a dog."

I couldn't take my eyes off her. "Thank goodness for that." Thank goodness for this big, messy family who brought us together. And then together again.

"Bah Humbug, Ethan."

"Merry Christmas, Marlowe."

Epilogue

Marlowe

December, One Year Later

Light applause sounded as members of the Holly family and the community gathered before a shiny red ribbon stretched across the front porch steps of Hollybrooke House.

So much had happened in one simple year. We'd established a family trust for the house. Created a separate Holly Family Foundation as a non-profit charitable organization to support community needs, including the transition of the Hollybrooke House into a family services respite facility.

As a seasoned community board member, Brianne had been a rock star throughout. Her connections and knowledge of board structure became invaluable. Even Shawn had to concede she, in fact, had better business sense than him. A statement the entire family witnessed over dinner last night, as follow-through on the wager he'd made with Brianne over beers at Checkers early in our foundation planning. We got it on video.

Sheree Bolden spoke to the crowd, thanking those present for their help and support. "Services to support families are vital for a community to thrive."

She'd been on-site weekly to check progress on renovations. The house now included a ramp entry at the side door from the driveway, several widened doorways, and modifications to the ground floor bathroom to ensure the house met guidelines from the Americans with Disabilities Act.

Money we raised with the foundation went to many of these costs, requiring constant fundraising efforts. It was all a bit overwhelming. Just kidding. It was freaking amazing. Data all day, baby. I split my time between remote part-time work for a data analytics company head-quartered in Chicago, and working on the foundation and overseeing the renovations alongside Sheree.

Sheree turned to me. "Marlowe. I believe you should be the one to cut the ribbon."

We'd discussed this moment ahead of time, but the gesture still took me by surprise. She handed me a gleaming pair of silver scissors. I held in a breath. I couldn't describe in words how much this moment meant. How much being here, surrounded by family and both new and familiar faces, gave me purpose. Gave me hope.

Not to delay this shindig further, I gave the pristine ribbon a decisive snip.

Applause sounded again. Ashe whistled and Cara whooped, "Woohoo!"

Riley snapped photos while Rafe made rounds through the crowd, schmoozing his business contacts. My nieces and nephews chatted with kids and their families. This project brought all of us together in a way none of us expected. Well, none but Grans.

Seated in one of the few chairs we'd brought outdoors for the occasion, Grans stood to lead guests into the home.

Ethan circled around the crowd to my side. "Way to go, Marlowe. Arlene is already spreading word on the town online forum about how beautiful the house looks."

I glanced past him. "She hasn't even gone inside yet."

He shrugged. "Good press is good press." He held out a hand. "Come on. Let's head in."

The house still held so many personal memories but had changed enough to feel like a space that no longer belonged to me. The front parlor now housed kid-friendly tables and chairs, a bright, durable rug, and a comfy, modular couch. The library's broken doors had been removed and left open for accessibility. The built-in shelves were partly filled by books, board games, and puzzles. Many shelves sat bare, waiting to be filled once we grew our funding. Grans' office now functioned as a first-floor bedroom with a widened doorway for wheelchair access.

The dining hall held our family table, donated by Grans. The thing was massive. A lighter shade of wall paint added a brightness to the room.

Ethan hooked into my arm and steered me into the kitchen, where a section of wall no longer existed for wider access to the hall and back sitting room.

He spoke low into my ear. "I have good memories of this room. A vision of you dusted in flour."

I swatted him. "That was so embarrassing. For me."

"Was it? I thought it was hot."

I took in a sharp breath of air. "*I* thought it was hot." I'd never admitted it to him. "You stood so close I could only hold my breath as you wiped the smeared flour off my face. I think that's when I knew you were the one."

"Is that right?" He smoothed a hand against his trimmed beard. "I'm a real charmer in the kitchen."

I stole a quick kiss before anyone else came into the room. "That you are, Sawyer. Maybe I'll use it my vows."

Ethan stilled. "Your...vows?"

I grinned. "Okay, our vows."

He gawked at me.

"I'm giving you sufficient notice in case you have a Christmas Eve proposal in the works. Or Christmas Day?" I loved watching him squirm. We'd already discussed an engagement, so it wasn't as if the topic hadn't been brought up. The logistics of coordinating an engagement plus timing the wedding for the least busy but still optimal time of year gave me plenty to plan for. After seeing how my BFF Anna, now married in California, had organized an incredible outdoor wedding in six months, I had my work cut out for me. Best to get ahead of the game.

"I wouldn't have pegged you for a Christmas proposal kind of gal," he said in a careful tone.

"Creating new memories this time of year seemed like an idea you'd be into."

"True. But you don't like the holidays. The last thing—"

I pressed a finger to his lips. "Remember what I said at New Year's? I'm wiping the slate clean. No more humbuggery."

He smooched my finger before I removed it. "You already grumbled about the town's Christmas decorations going up the day after Halloween."

"Obviously. That's criminally early."

"Not for the second most popular Christmas destination in the state."

"Look, I didn't once complain about the Christmas in July stuff," I pointed out.

We progressed to the back family room. A Christmas tree stood by the window, courtesy of Sawyer and Sanderson Farms. Ethan brought it over two days ago. We'd decorated the tree with white lights and snowflake ornaments. The rest of the tree would be filled in by hand-made ornaments the kids planned to make during the first open session at Hollybrooke.

The room bustled with people. Gone from the mantle was our family portrait, now hung at Ashe and Cara's. The old clock in the corner had moved into storage until Grans' condo was ready to move into. She stayed with Uncle Joe and Aunt Sunny in the meantime.

Mayor Bennington approached. "Marlowe, will we see you at the Tasty Bake this year?"

A nervous laugh escaped. "Actually, I'm partnering with the Sawyers and Sandersons for their event at the farm. They expanded it with three food trucks this year, and more activities. My talents are best used outside of baking competitions. Or holiday obstacle courses."

The farm was on its way to meet Ethan's expansion plan. Trees took years to grow, so the merger with the Sanderson farm wouldn't yield new trees for a while. After securing a loan for upgrades, together with the Sandersons, Ethan reconfigured the front of the Sawyer property by the road for more streamlined traffic flow and parking. They hauled away the trailer office and constructed a new outbuilding with offices in the back. Built to look like a small barn, it served as a storefront for holiday decorations, farm branded T-shirts and other merch, and Ethan's woodwork. The store would stay open year-round. Meanwhile, they used the existing barn to create a larger woodworking area.

Most importantly, those pesky borrowed acres had new signatures on the deed, now belonging to Sawyer and Sanderson Farms.

"I'll be sure to visit the farm this season." Mayor Bennington glanced between us with a knowing smile. "It sounds like town square will be less...dramatic this season."

I spun to Ethan with my eyes widened after the mayor moved on. "See?" I whisper shouted. "People never forget!"

He held up a hand. "I swear, all family shenanigans will occur off of public property."

"How about no family shenanigans." Miracles could happen, right?

Ethan ran a hand up my back. A thrill sang inside me, even through my thick sweater. "Maybe I'll wait until Valentine's Day."

"To propose? You wouldn't dare."

"Did someone say propose?" Arlene, spreader of gossip, just happened to overhear. Light danced in her eyes as she waited on the deets.

I nudged Ethan with my boot. "The rumors are already flying."

Ethan kissed my cheek. "It's sweet you think you have any idea what I've already planned."

I gasped. "Ethan!"

He grinned. "This is going to be a fun month, Marlowe. I can't wait to see how surprised you're going to be."

"Did I tell you already today that I love you? Because I'm taking it back."

He swept me into his arms, seemingly oblivious to nosy town snoops or lurking nearby Hollys. "I know you love me. I love you right back. Just as I always have."

We kissed. Long enough to make my toes curl but short enough not to incite more town gossip.

Ethan pulled back, still holding on. "I had an idea."

"Please tell me it doesn't involve a contest or a cookbook."

"It involves a hill, some trees, and a wooden arch with flowers."

My nose scrunched. "That's quite a riddle."

"The area on the western edge of the property? It could make a really nice spot for an outdoor wedding."

I knew exactly where he meant. And I could visualize it instantly. I squeezed his arms. "Ethan. It's perfect."

"Could be a new revenue stream for the farm if we play it right."

"But we should be the first." A wedding venue! Ideas flew through my mind. "If we clear that area past the storefront—look, I'm going to need a spreadsheet." I made a move to take off and Ethan gently tugged me toward him.

"In time," he said. "Come on, let's get a photo by the tree. For the memory book."

We'd been adding to it all year. So much so, that we would soon run out of blank pages. I had that covered too, with a new photo album to gift Ethan this Christmas.

Ethan snapped a selfie of us. I couldn't wait to make more memories.

Thank you for reading Miss Humbug! I hope you enjoyed Marlowe and Ethan's story. Ready for more sweet romance? Check out my books and author email list at stephaniejscott.com

Acknowledgements

Research for writing a holiday romance requires the burden of consuming holiday movies and romance books (it's a rough gig, but someone has to do it – armed with hot cocoa and heated blankets). Truly though, it's a joy to write comfort books and I hope to write many more.

Thank you, as always, to my regular crew of writer friends: Kelly Garcia, Vanessa M. Knight, Jen Bailey, and Robin Kuss, who make plotting fun. (Okay, less painful.) Big thanks to Kasey Kennedy for her sharp eye for continuity. To Chicago North Romance Writers for support and insight. To my new and my regular ARC readers: I appreciate you so much. Your enthusiasm helps keep me focused in the final stretch.

Also By Stephanie J. Scott

Miss Humbug
OMG Christmas Tree
Lady and the Camp
Falling Into Place

Young Adult Books

All Last Summer
Sunset Summer
Big Wild Summer
Free Wheeling Summer
All-Star Love
Alterations

About the Author

Stephanie J. Scott writes light-hearted, quirky romance and young adult. She enjoys dance fitness, everything cats, and has a slight obsession with Instagram. A Midwest girl at heart, she resides outside of Chicago with her tech-of-all-trades husband and fuzzy furbabies.

Photo: Leah Lewis Photography